GRAPHIC NOVEL CLASSICS

SHERLOCK HOLMES
THE
HOUND OF THE BASKERVILLES

SIR ARTHUR CONAN DOYLE
AND CLAIRE BAMPTON

PowerKiDS press

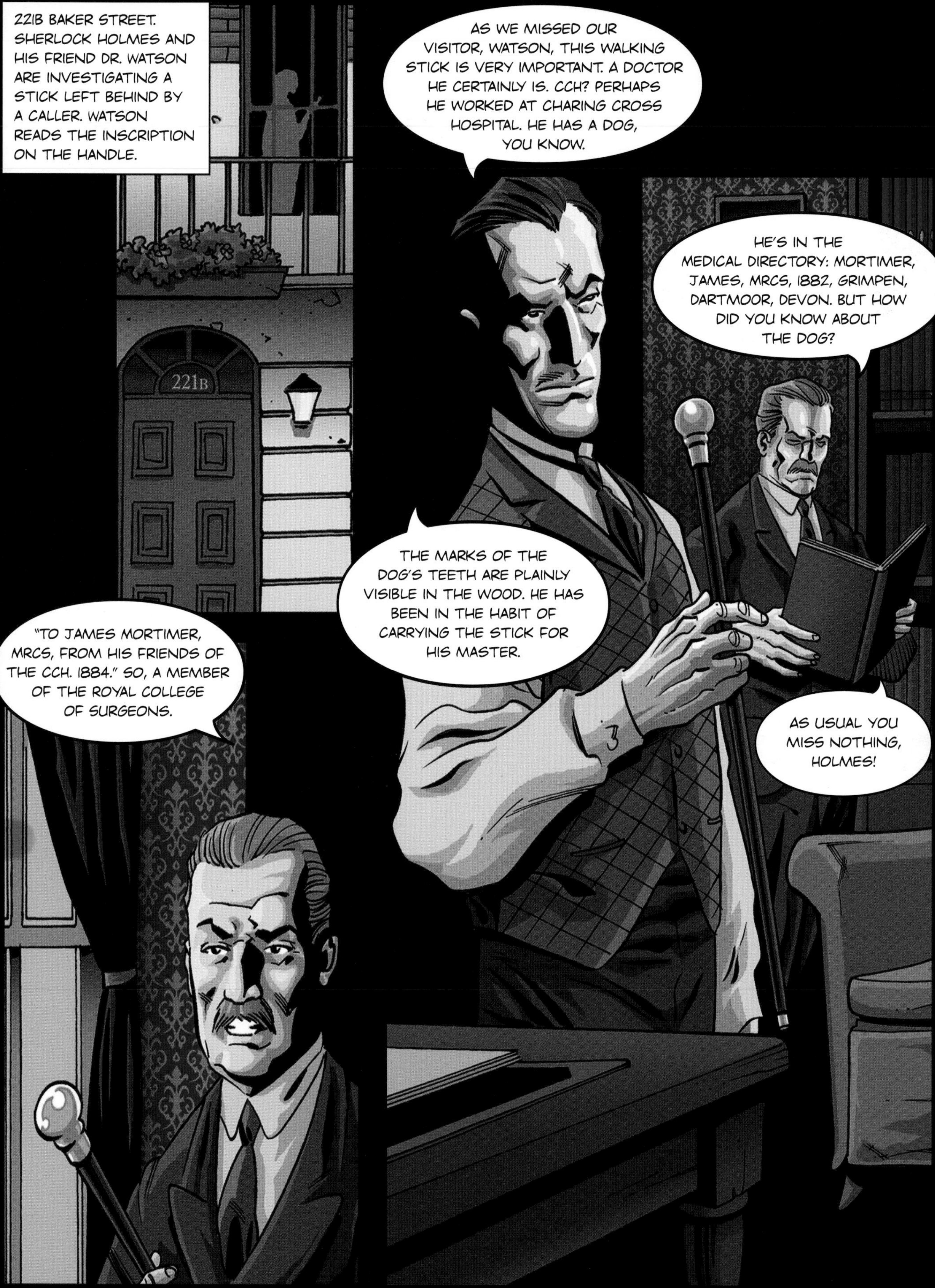
221B BAKER STREET. SHERLOCK HOLMES AND HIS FRIEND DR. WATSON ARE INVESTIGATING A STICK LEFT BEHIND BY A CALLER. WATSON READS THE INSCRIPTION ON THE HANDLE.
221B
AS WE MISSED OUR VISITOR, WATSON, THIS WALKING STICK IS VERY IMPORTANT. A DOCTOR HE CERTAINLY IS. CCH? PERHAPS HE WORKED AT CHARING CROSS HOSPITAL. HE HAS A DOG, YOU KNOW.
HE'S IN THE MEDICAL DIRECTORY: MORTIMER, JAMES, MRCS, 1882, GRIMPEN, DARTMOOR, DEVON. BUT HOW DID YOU KNOW ABOUT THE DOG?
"TO JAMES MORTIMER, MRCS, FROM HIS FRIENDS OF THE CCH. 1884." SO, A MEMBER OF THE ROYAL COLLEGE OF SURGEONS.
THE MARKS OF THE DOG'S TEETH ARE PLAINLY VISIBLE IN THE WOOD. HE HAS BEEN IN THE HABIT OF CARRYING THE STICK FOR HIS MASTER.
AS USUAL YOU MISS NOTHING, HOLMES!

AND THE DOG'S OWNER IS APPROACHING OUR DOOR. I WONDER WHAT THIS MAN OF SCIENCE WANTS FROM A SPECIALIST IN CRIME.
A MAN WITH A DOG PUSHES HIS WAY THROUGH THE CROWD AND RINGS AT THE DOOR OF 221B BAKER STREET.
DR. JAMES MORTIMER?
MISTER, SIR, MISTER, A HUMBLE MRSC - A MERE DABBLER IN SCIENCE AND YOU ARE SHERLOCK HOLMES, I PRESUME?
YES INDEED. PLEASE COME IN AND MEET MY FRIEND DR. WATSON.
SO WHAT EXACTLY IS THE NATURE OF YOUR PROBLEM?
I HAVE HERE A MANUSCRIPT DATED 1742. IT WAS COMMITTED TO MY CARE BY SIR CHARLES BASKERVILLE OF BASKERVILLE HALL IN DARTMOUTH, DEVON. HE WAS A DEAR FRIEND WHO DIED TRAGICALLY JUST THREE MONTHS AGO. WITH YOUR PERMISSION, I SHOULD LIKE TO READ IT OUT TO YOU.
CERTAINLY, MY GOOD FELLOW. PLEASE DO.

AND SO MORTIMER BEGINS TO READ IN A HIGH, CRACKLING VOICE THE FOLLOWING CURIOUS, OLD-WORLD NARRATIVE...
"THIS IS THE STORY OF THE HOUND OF THE BASKERVILLES. I HEARD IT DIRECTLY FROM MY FATHER, AND HAVE SET IT DOWN EXACTLY AS IT WAS TOLD. IT BEGINS WITH HUGO BASKERVILLE, MY FATHER'S FATHER..."

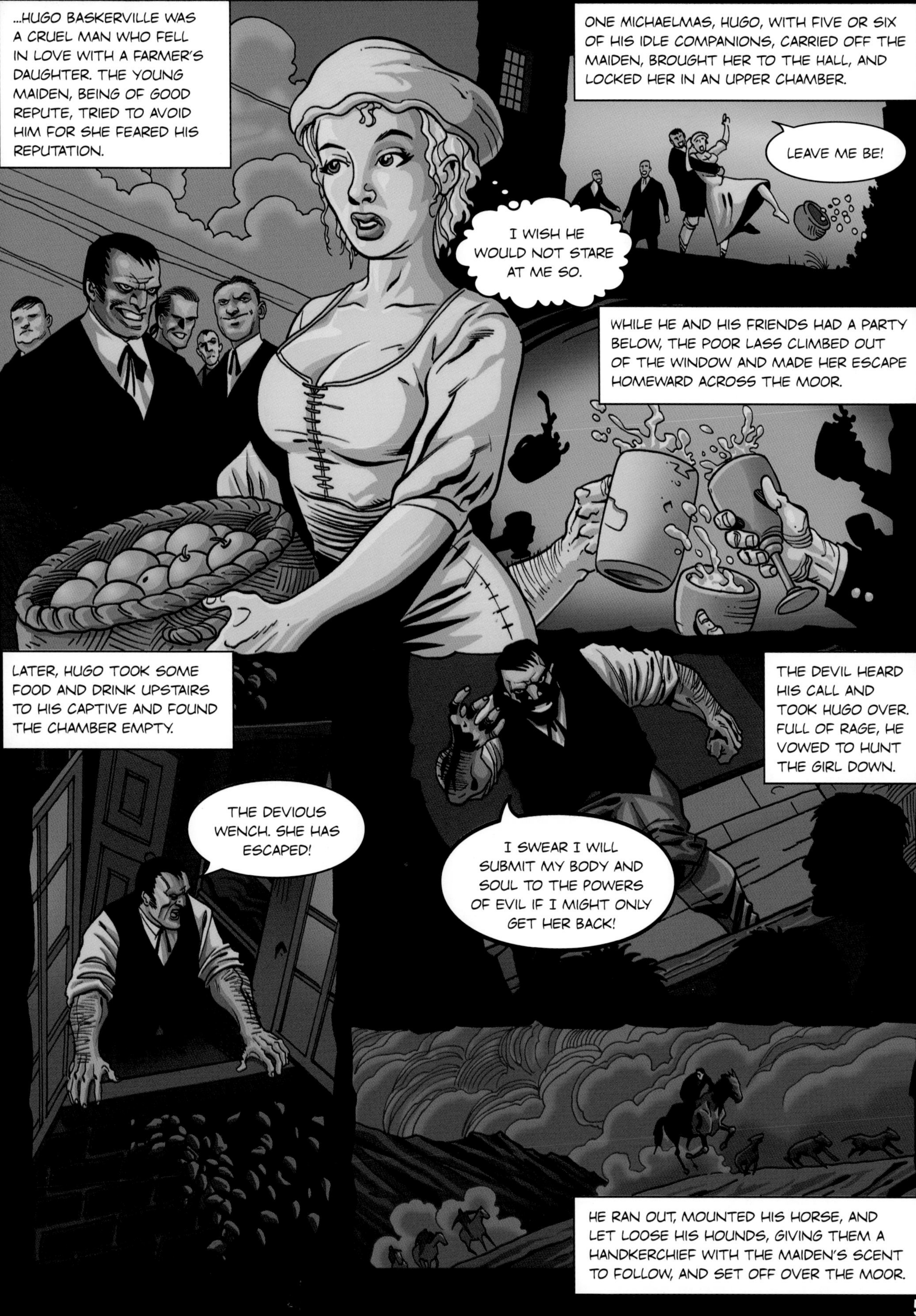

...HUGO BASKERVILLE WAS A CRUEL MAN WHO FELL IN LOVE WITH A FARMER'S DAUGHTER. THE YOUNG MAIDEN, BEING OF GOOD REPUTE, TRIED TO AVOID HIM FOR SHE FEARED HIS REPUTATION.
I WISH HE WOULD NOT STARE AT ME SO.
ONE MICHAELMAS, HUGO, WITH FIVE OR SIX OF HIS IDLE COMPANIONS, CARRIED OFF THE MAIDEN, BROUGHT HER TO THE HALL, AND LOCKED HER IN AN UPPER CHAMBER.
LEAVE ME BE!
WHILE HE AND HIS FRIENDS HAD A PARTY BELOW, THE POOR LASS CLIMBED OUT OF THE WINDOW AND MADE HER ESCAPE HOMEWARD ACROSS THE MOOR.
LATER, HUGO TOOK SOME FOOD AND DRINK UPSTAIRS TO HIS CAPTIVE AND FOUND THE CHAMBER EMPTY.
THE DEVIOUS WENCH. SHE HAS ESCAPED!
I SWEAR I WILL SUBMIT MY BODY AND SOUL TO THE POWERS OF EVIL IF I MIGHT ONLY GET HER BACK!
THE DEVIL HEARD HIS CALL AND TOOK HUGO OVER. FULL OF RAGE, HE VOWED TO HUNT THE GIRL DOWN.
HE RAN OUT, MOUNTED HIS HORSE, AND LET LOOSE HIS HOUNDS, GIVING THEM A HANDKERCHIEF WITH THE MAIDEN'S SCENT TO FOLLOW, AND SET OFF OVER THE MOOR.

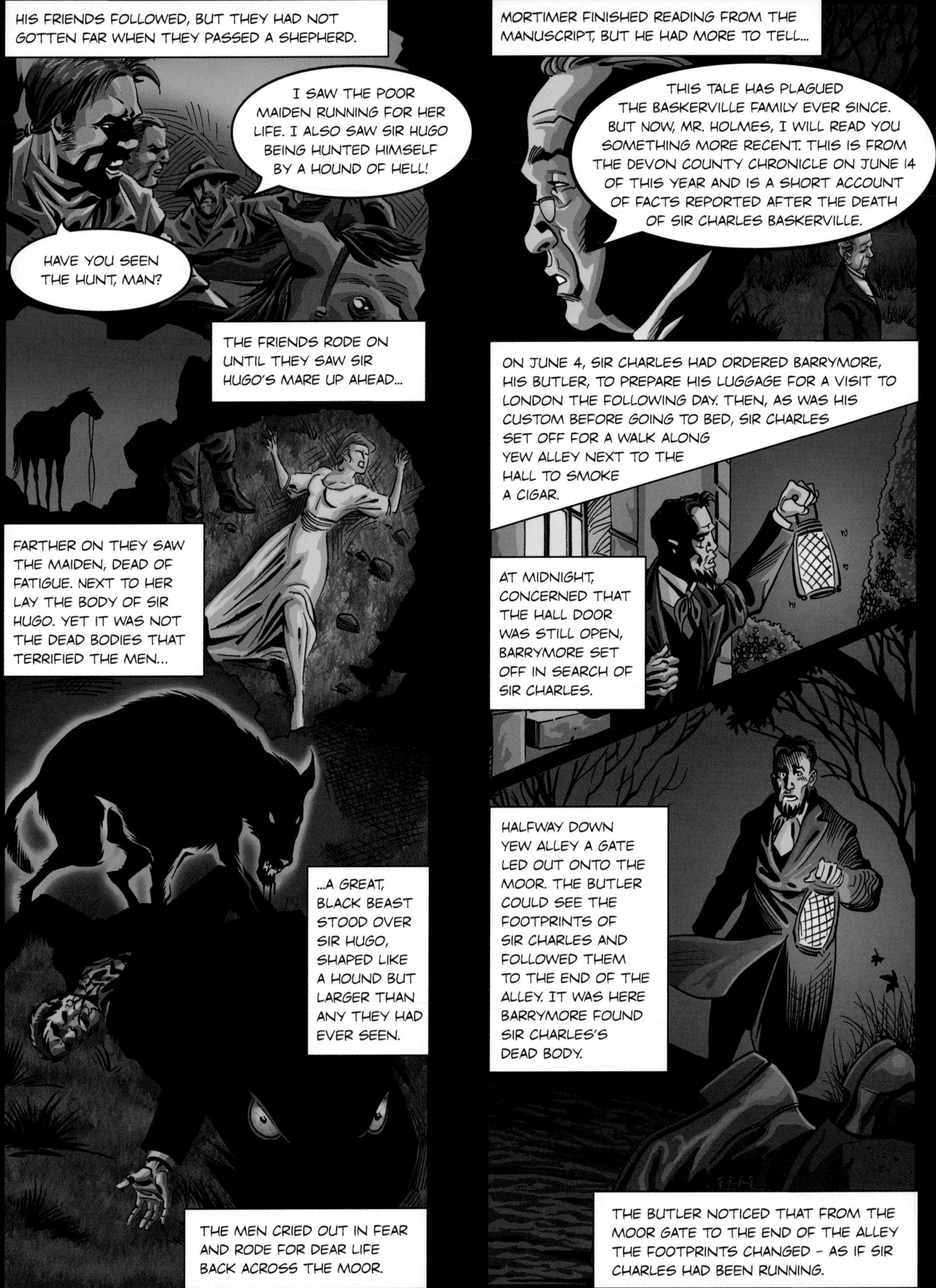
HIS FRIENDS FOLLOWED, BUT THEY HAD NOT GOTTEN FAR WHEN THEY PASSED A SHEPHERD.
HAVE YOU SEEN THE HUNT, MAN?
I SAW THE POOR MAIDEN RUNNING FOR HER LIFE. I ALSO SAW SIR HUGO BEING HUNTED HIMSELF BY A HOUND OF HELL!
THE FRIENDS RODE ON UNTIL THEY SAW SIR HUGO'S MARE UP AHEAD...
FARTHER ON THEY SAW THE MAIDEN, DEAD OF FATIGUE. NEXT TO HER LAY THE BODY OF SIR HUGO. YET IT WAS NOT THE DEAD BODIES THAT TERRIFIED THE MEN...
...A GREAT, BLACK BEAST STOOD OVER SIR HUGO, SHAPED LIKE A HOUND BUT LARGER THAN ANY THEY HAD EVER SEEN.
THE MEN CRIED OUT IN FEAR AND RODE FOR DEAR LIFE BACK ACROSS THE MOOR.
MORTIMER FINISHED READING FROM THE MANUSCRIPT, BUT HE HAD MORE TO TELL...
THIS TALE HAS PLAGUED THE BASKERVILLE FAMILY EVER SINCE. BUT NOW, MR. HOLMES, I WILL READ YOU SOMETHING MORE RECENT. THIS IS FROM THE DEVON COUNTY CHRONICLE ON JUNE 14 OF THIS YEAR AND IS A SHORT ACCOUNT OF FACTS REPORTED AFTER THE DEATH OF SIR CHARLES BASKERVILLE.
ON JUNE 4, SIR CHARLES HAD ORDERED BARRYMORE, HIS BUTLER, TO PREPARE HIS LUGGAGE FOR A VISIT TO LONDON THE FOLLOWING DAY. THEN, AS WAS HIS CUSTOM BEFORE GOING TO BED, SIR CHARLES SET OFF FOR A WALK ALONG YEW ALLEY NEXT TO THE HALL TO SMOKE A CIGAR.
AT MIDNIGHT, CONCERNED THAT THE HALL DOOR WAS STILL OPEN, BARRYMORE SET OFF IN SEARCH OF SIR CHARLES.
HALFWAY DOWN YEW ALLEY A GATE LED OUT ONTO THE MOOR. THE BUTLER COULD SEE THE FOOTPRINTS OF SIR CHARLES AND FOLLOWED THEM TO THE END OF THE ALLEY. IT WAS HERE BARRYMORE FOUND SIR CHARLES'S DEAD BODY.
THE BUTLER NOTICED THAT FROM THE MOOR GATE TO THE END OF THE ALLEY THE FOOTPRINTS CHANGED – AS IF SIR CHARLES HAD BEEN RUNNING.

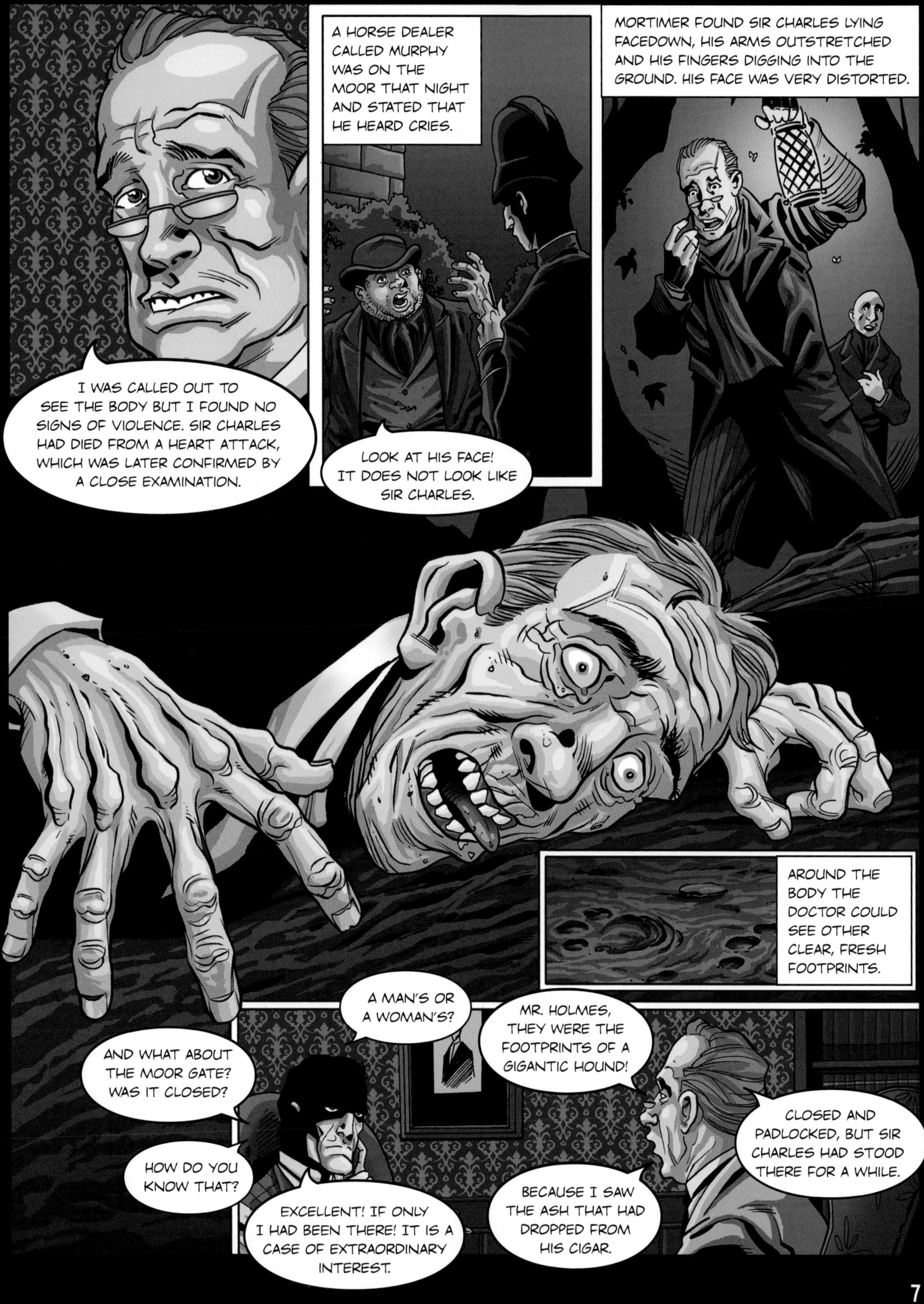
I WAS CALLED OUT TO SEE THE BODY BUT I FOUND NO SIGNS OF VIOLENCE. SIR CHARLES HAD DIED FROM A HEART ATTACK, WHICH WAS LATER CONFIRMED BY A CLOSE EXAMINATION.
A HORSE DEALER CALLED MURPHY WAS ON THE MOOR THAT NIGHT AND STATED THAT HE HEARD CRIES.
LOOK AT HIS FACE! IT DOES NOT LOOK LIKE SIR CHARLES.
MORTIMER FOUND SIR CHARLES LYING FACEDOWN, HIS ARMS OUTSTRETCHED AND HIS FINGERS DIGGING INTO THE GROUND. HIS FACE WAS VERY DISTORTED.
AROUND THE BODY THE DOCTOR COULD SEE OTHER CLEAR, FRESH FOOTPRINTS.
A MAN'S OR A WOMAN'S?
MR. HOLMES, THEY WERE THE FOOTPRINTS OF A GIGANTIC HOUND!
AND WHAT ABOUT THE MOOR GATE? WAS IT CLOSED?
CLOSED AND PADLOCKED, BUT SIR CHARLES HAD STOOD THERE FOR A WHILE.
HOW DO YOU KNOW THAT?
BECAUSE I SAW THE ASH THAT HAD DROPPED FROM HIS CIGAR.
EXCELLENT! IF ONLY I HAD BEEN THERE! IT IS A CASE OF EXTRAORDINARY INTEREST.

BUT THERE IS A REALM IN WHICH EVEN THE MOST EXPERIENCED OF DETECTIVES IS HELPLESS. I HAVE DISCOVERED THAT BEFORE THE TERRIBLE EVENT OCCURRED, SEVERAL PEOPLE HAD SEEN A CREATURE ON THE MOOR - A GHASTLY CREATURE, LUMINOUS AND SPECTRAL. A SUPERNATURAL APPARITION THAT SOUNDS EXACTLY LIKE THE HOUND OF THE BASKERVILLES LEGEND.

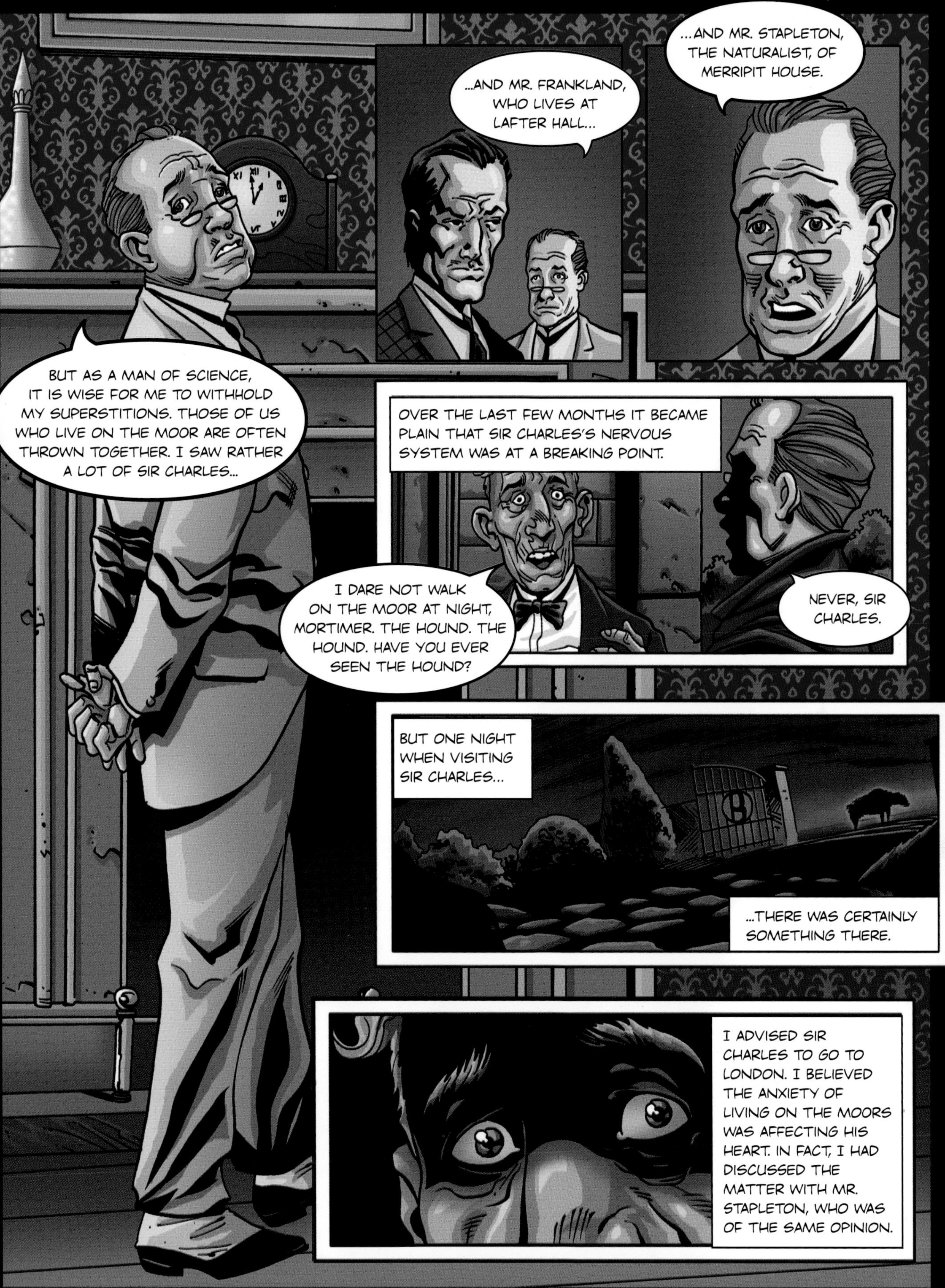

...AND MR. FRANKLAND, WHO LIVES AT LAFTER HALL...
...AND MR. STAPLETON, THE NATURALIST, OF MERRIPIT HOUSE.
BUT AS A MAN OF SCIENCE, IT IS WISE FOR ME TO WITHHOLD MY SUPERSTITIONS. THOSE OF US WHO LIVE ON THE MOOR ARE OFTEN THROWN TOGETHER. I SAW RATHER A LOT OF SIR CHARLES...
OVER THE LAST FEW MONTHS IT BECAME PLAIN THAT SIR CHARLES'S NERVOUS SYSTEM WAS AT A BREAKING POINT.
I DARE NOT WALK ON THE MOOR AT NIGHT, MORTIMER. THE HOUND. THE HOUND. HAVE YOU EVER SEEN THE HOUND?
NEVER, SIR CHARLES.
BUT ONE NIGHT WHEN VISITING SIR CHARLES...
...THERE WAS CERTAINLY SOMETHING THERE.
I ADVISED SIR CHARLES TO GO TO LONDON. I BELIEVED THE ANXIETY OF LIVING ON THE MOORS WAS AFFECTING HIS HEART. IN FACT, I HAD DISCUSSED THE MATTER WITH MR. STAPLETON, WHO WAS OF THE SAME OPINION.

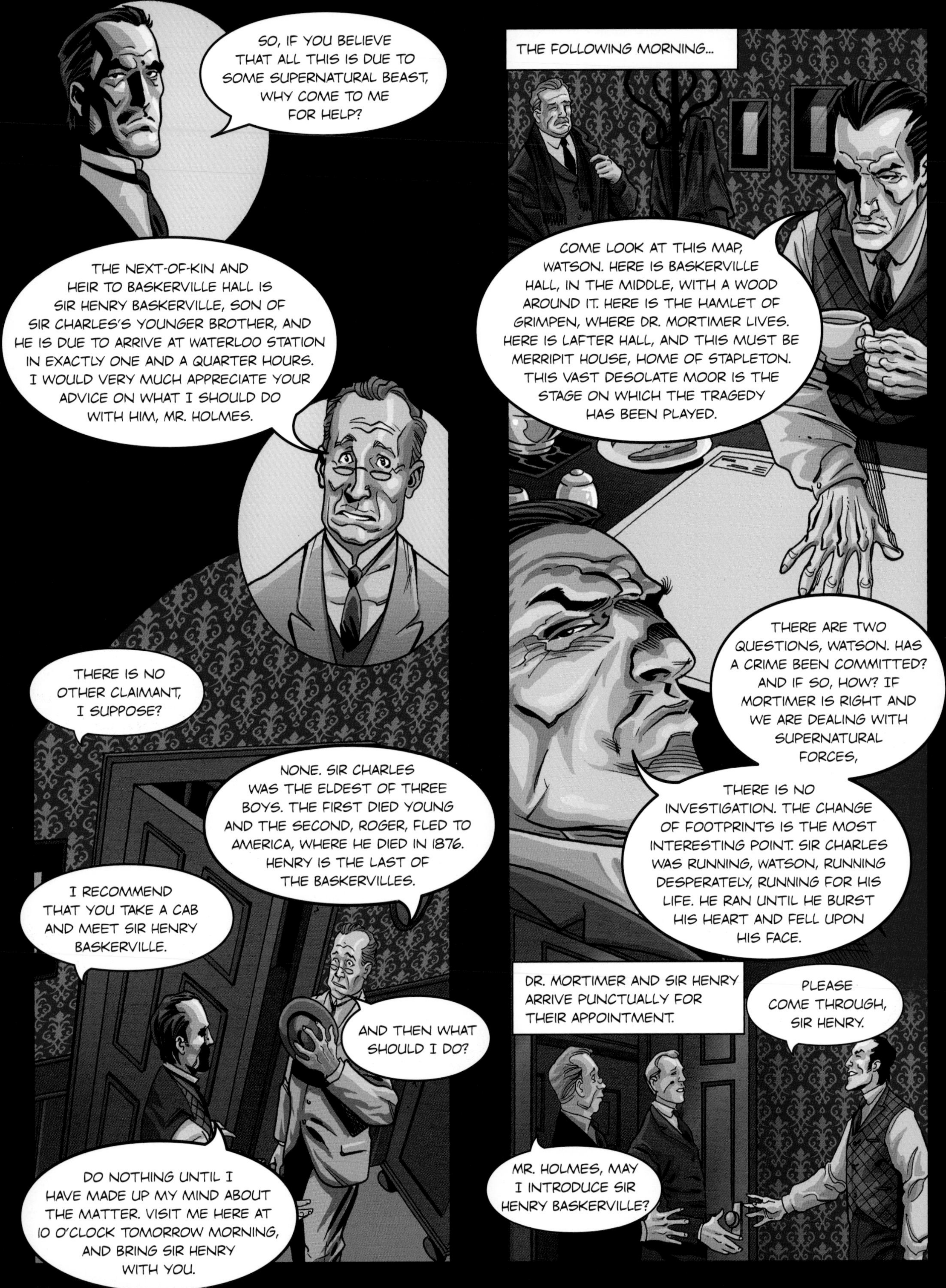
SO, IF YOU BELIEVE THAT ALL THIS IS DUE TO SOME SUPERNATURAL BEAST, WHY COME TO ME FOR HELP?
THE NEXT-OF-KIN AND HEIR TO BASKERVILLE HALL IS SIR HENRY BASKERVILLE, SON OF SIR CHARLES'S YOUNGER BROTHER, AND HE IS DUE TO ARRIVE AT WATERLOO STATION IN EXACTLY ONE AND A QUARTER HOURS. I WOULD VERY MUCH APPRECIATE YOUR ADVICE ON WHAT I SHOULD DO WITH HIM, MR. HOLMES.
THERE IS NO OTHER CLAIMANT, I SUPPOSE?
NONE. SIR CHARLES WAS THE ELDEST OF THREE BOYS. THE FIRST DIED YOUNG AND THE SECOND, ROGER, FLED TO AMERICA, WHERE HE DIED IN 1876. HENRY IS THE LAST OF THE BASKERVILLES.
I RECOMMEND THAT YOU TAKE A CAB AND MEET SIR HENRY BASKERVILLE.
AND THEN WHAT SHOULD I DO?
DO NOTHING UNTIL I HAVE MADE UP MY MIND ABOUT THE MATTER. VISIT ME HERE AT 10 O'CLOCK TOMORROW MORNING, AND BRING SIR HENRY WITH YOU.
THE FOLLOWING MORNING...
COME LOOK AT THIS MAP, WATSON. HERE IS BASKERVILLE HALL, IN THE MIDDLE, WITH A WOOD AROUND IT. HERE IS THE HAMLET OF GRIMPEN, WHERE DR. MORTIMER LIVES. HERE IS LAFTER HALL, AND THIS MUST BE MERRIPIT HOUSE, HOME OF STAPLETON. THIS VAST DESOLATE MOOR IS THE STAGE ON WHICH THE TRAGEDY HAS BEEN PLAYED.
THERE ARE TWO QUESTIONS, WATSON. HAS A CRIME BEEN COMMITTED? AND IF SO, HOW? IF MORTIMER IS RIGHT AND WE ARE DEALING WITH SUPERNATURAL FORCES,
THERE IS NO INVESTIGATION. THE CHANGE OF FOOTPRINTS IS THE MOST INTERESTING POINT. SIR CHARLES WAS RUNNING, WATSON, RUNNING DESPERATELY, RUNNING FOR HIS LIFE. HE RAN UNTIL HE BURST HIS HEART AND FELL UPON HIS FACE.
DR. MORTIMER AND SIR HENRY ARRIVE PUNCTUALLY FOR THEIR APPOINTMENT.
PLEASE COME THROUGH, SIR HENRY.
MR. HOLMES, MAY I INTRODUCE SIR HENRY BASKERVILLE?

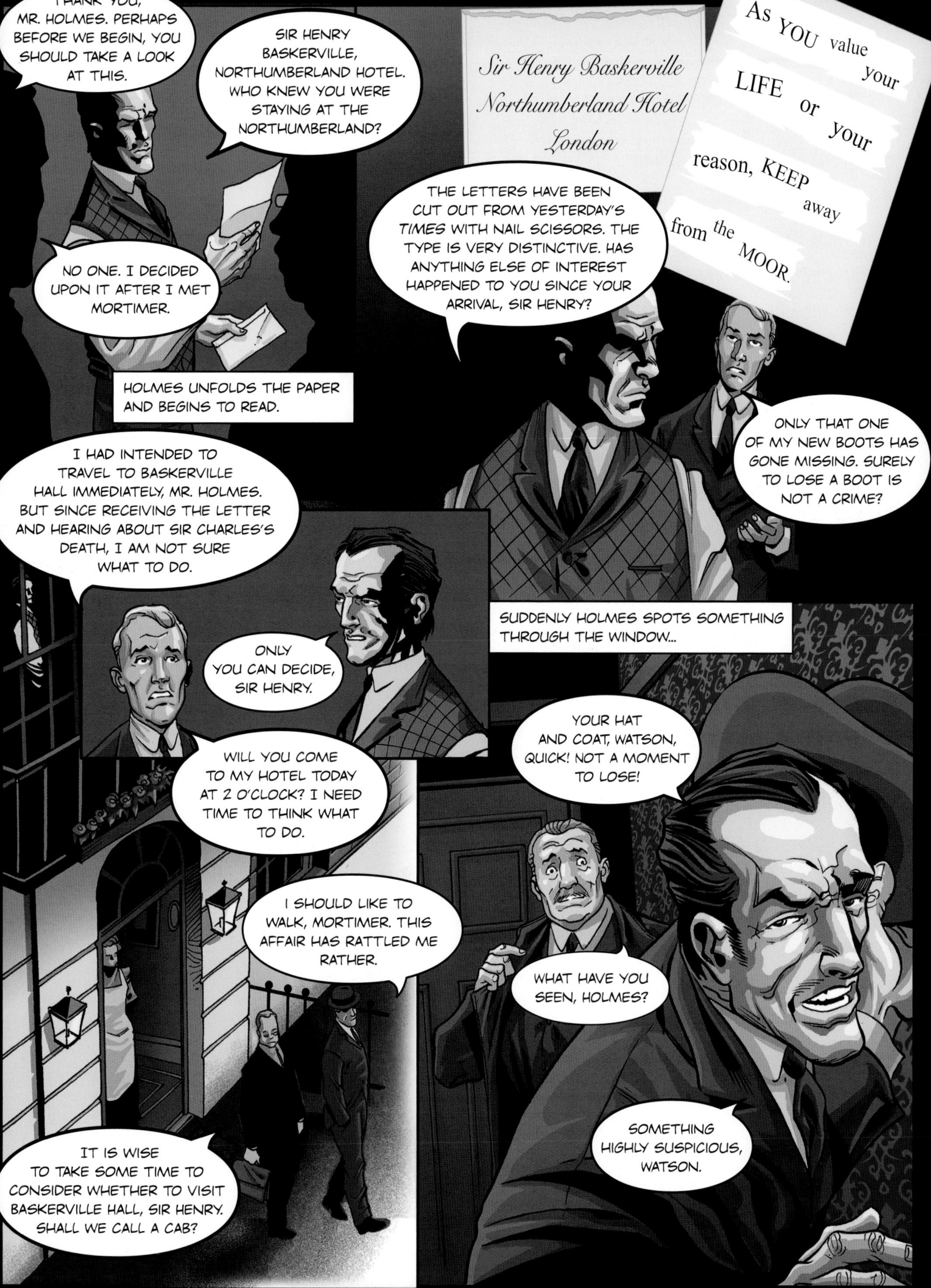

THANK YOU, MR. HOLMES. PERHAPS BEFORE WE BEGIN, YOU SHOULD TAKE A LOOK AT THIS.
SIR HENRY BASKERVILLE, NORTHUMBERLAND HOTEL. WHO KNEW YOU WERE STAYING AT THE NORTHUMBERLAND?
Sir Henry Baskerville Northumberland Hotel London
As YOU value your LIFE or your reason, KEEP away from the MOOR.
NO ONE. I DECIDED UPON IT AFTER I MET MORTIMER.
HOLMES UNFOLDS THE PAPER AND BEGINS TO READ.
THE LETTERS HAVE BEEN CUT OUT FROM YESTERDAY'S *TIMES* WITH NAIL SCISSORS. THE TYPE IS VERY DISTINCTIVE. HAS ANYTHING ELSE OF INTEREST HAPPENED TO YOU SINCE YOUR ARRIVAL, SIR HENRY?
ONLY THAT ONE OF MY NEW BOOTS HAS GONE MISSING. SURELY TO LOSE A BOOT IS NOT A CRIME?
I HAD INTENDED TO TRAVEL TO BASKERVILLE HALL IMMEDIATELY, MR. HOLMES. BUT SINCE RECEIVING THE LETTER AND HEARING ABOUT SIR CHARLES'S DEATH, I AM NOT SURE WHAT TO DO.
ONLY YOU CAN DECIDE, SIR HENRY.
WILL YOU COME TO MY HOTEL TODAY AT 2 O'CLOCK? I NEED TIME TO THINK WHAT TO DO.
I SHOULD LIKE TO WALK, MORTIMER. THIS AFFAIR HAS RATTLED ME RATHER.
IT IS WISE TO TAKE SOME TIME TO CONSIDER WHETHER TO VISIT BASKERVILLE HALL, SIR HENRY. SHALL WE CALL A CAB?
SUDDENLY HOLMES SPOTS SOMETHING THROUGH THE WINDOW...
YOUR HAT AND COAT, WATSON, QUICK! NOT A MOMENT TO LOSE!
WHAT HAVE YOU SEEN, HOLMES?
SOMETHING HIGHLY SUSPICIOUS, WATSON.

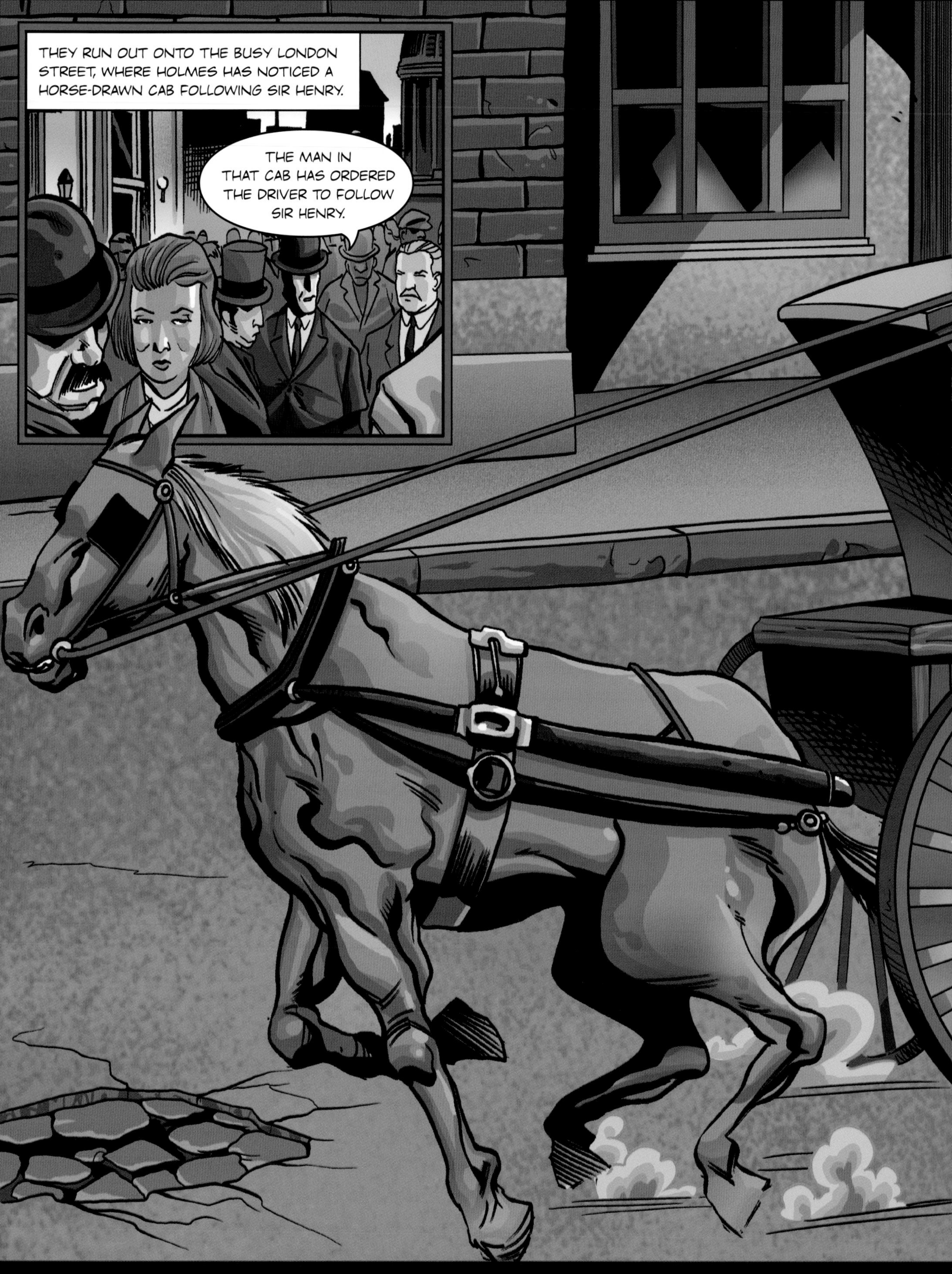
THEY RUN OUT ONTO THE BUSY LONDON STREET, WHERE HOLMES HAS NOTICED A HORSE-DRAWN CAB FOLLOWING SIR HENRY.
THE MAN IN THAT CAB HAS ORDERED THE DRIVER TO FOLLOW SIR HENRY.

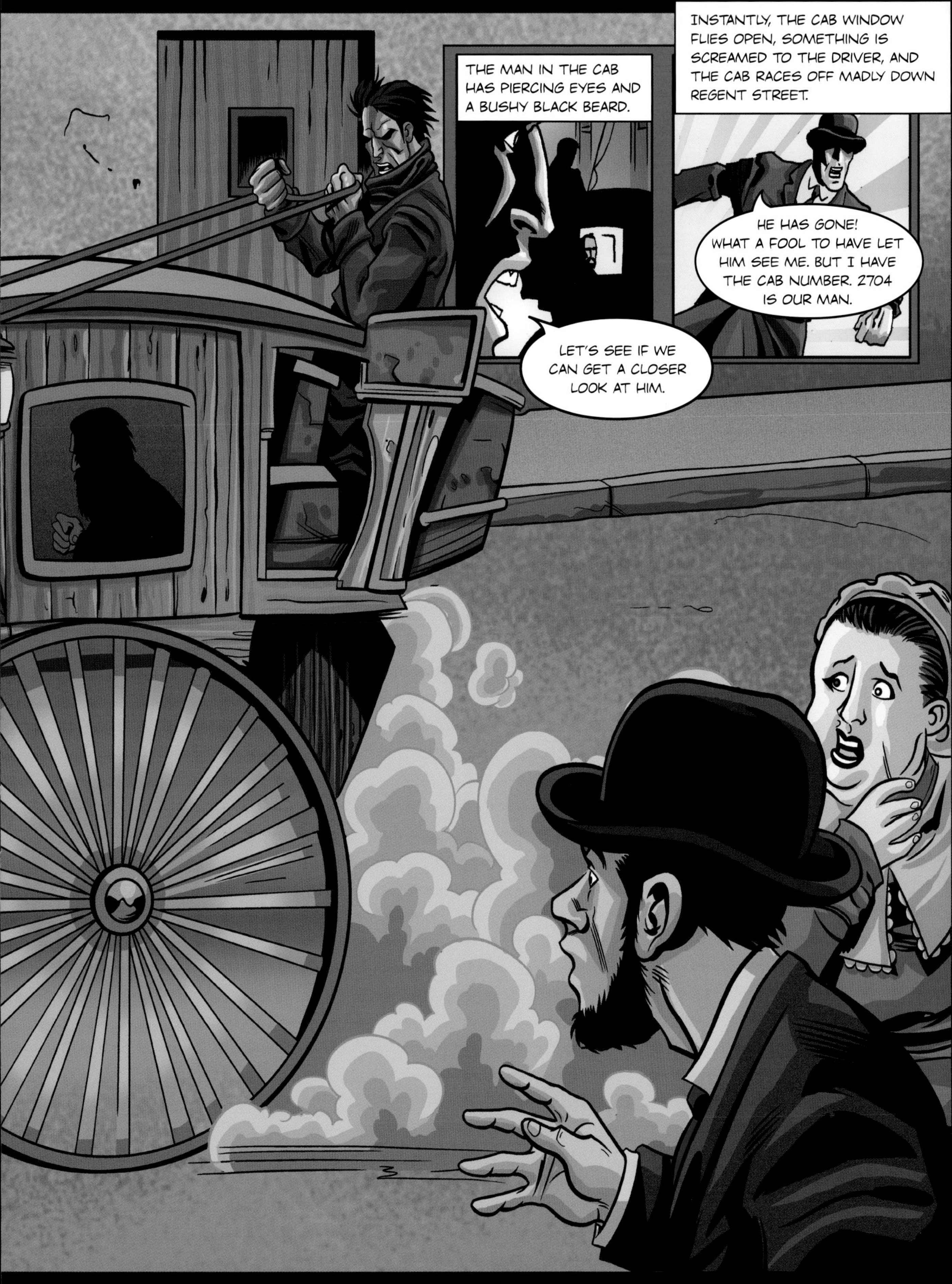

THE MAN IN THE CAB HAS PIERCING EYES AND A BUSHY BLACK BEARD.
LET'S SEE IF WE CAN GET A CLOSER LOOK AT HIM.
INSTANTLY, THE CAB WINDOW FLIES OPEN, SOMETHING IS SCREAMED TO THE DRIVER, AND THE CAB RACES OFF MADLY DOWN REGENT STREET.
HE HAS GONE! WHAT A FOOL TO HAVE LET HIM SEE ME. BUT I HAVE THE CAB NUMBER. 2704 IS OUR MAN.

LATER THAT AFTERNOON, AT THE NORTHUMBERLAND HOTEL...
THEY ARE PLAYING ME FOR A FOOL IN THIS HOTEL. I CAN TAKE A JOKE, BUT THIS TIME THEY'VE GONE TOO FAR.
STILL LOOKING FOR YOUR BOOT?
YES, AND NOW ANOTHER ONE HAS GONE MISSING. YESTERDAY THEY TOOK ONE OF MY NEW BROWN BOOTS. TODAY IT'S ONE OF MY OLD BLACK ONES THAT HAS VANISHED.
INTERESTING, SIR HENRY. VERY INTERESTING.
I HAVE DECIDED TO GO TO BASKERVILLE HALL, MR. HOLMES.
ON THE WHOLE I THINK YOUR DECISION WISE. DID YOU KNOW YOU WERE FOLLOWED THIS MORNING?
FOLLOWED?! BY WHOM?
I DON'T KNOW. MORTIMER, DO ANY OF THE MEN WHO LIVE NEAR YOU ON DARTMOOR HAVE A FULL BLACK BEARD?
NO - WAIT, YES - BARRYMORE, SIR CHARLES'S BUTLER. BUT HE IS IN DARTMOOR, IN CHARGE OF THE HALL.
DID BARRYMORE PROFIT AT ALL BY SIR CHARLES'S WILL?
HE AND HIS WIFE WERE LEFT 500 POUNDS EACH. THEY WERE AWARE THEY WOULD RECEIVE THIS AS SIR CHARLES WAS VERY FOND OF TALKING ABOUT HIS WILL.
I ALSO HAD 1,000 POUNDS LEFT TO ME.
INTERESTING. I WILL SEND A TELEGRAM TO BARRYMORE AT BASKERVILLE HALL AND ASK FOR IT TO BE RETURNED IF HE IS ABSENT. THAT SHOULD LET US KNOW WHETHER BARRYMORE IS IN DEVON OR NOT.
AND NOW, WATSON. ARE YOU PREPARED TO ACCOMPANY SIR HENRY TO BASKERVILLE HALL?
CERTAINLY, HOLMES. SHALL WE SAY 10 O'CLOCK ON SATURDAY AT PADDINGTON STATION?
INCREDIBLE! MY MISSING BROWN BOOT! BUT I SWEAR IT WAS NOT HERE BEFORE LUNCH. NOW TO FIND THE OLD BLACK ONE...

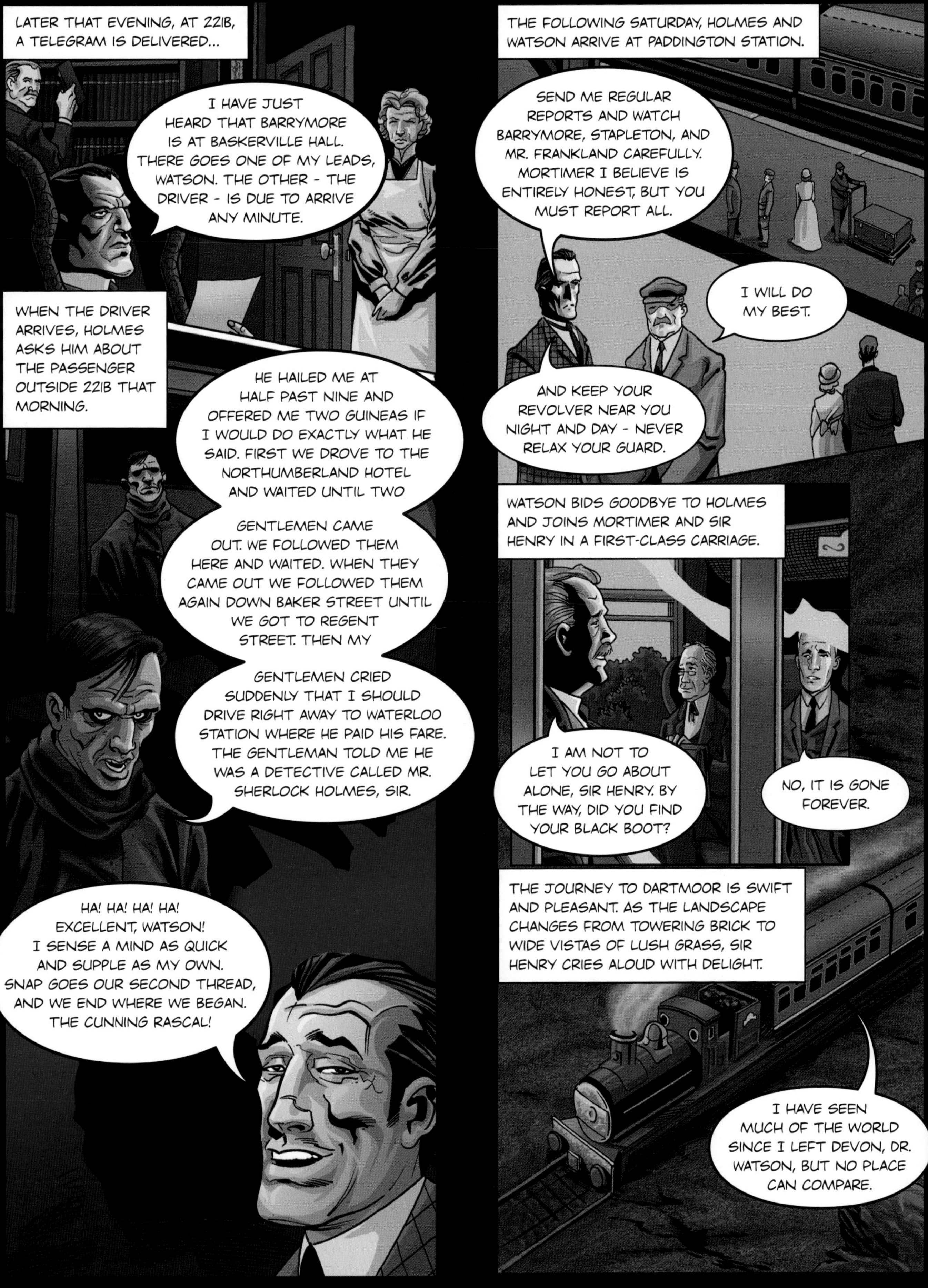
LATER THAT EVENING, AT 221B, A TELEGRAM IS DELIVERED...
I HAVE JUST HEARD THAT BARRYMORE IS AT BASKERVILLE HALL. THERE GOES ONE OF MY LEADS, WATSON. THE OTHER - THE DRIVER - IS DUE TO ARRIVE ANY MINUTE.
WHEN THE DRIVER ARRIVES, HOLMES ASKS HIM ABOUT THE PASSENGER OUTSIDE 221B THAT MORNING.
HE HAILED ME AT HALF PAST NINE AND OFFERED ME TWO GUINEAS IF I WOULD DO EXACTLY WHAT HE SAID. FIRST WE DROVE TO THE NORTHUMBERLAND HOTEL AND WAITED UNTIL TWO
GENTLEMEN CAME OUT. WE FOLLOWED THEM HERE AND WAITED. WHEN THEY CAME OUT WE FOLLOWED THEM AGAIN DOWN BAKER STREET UNTIL WE GOT TO REGENT STREET. THEN MY
GENTLEMEN CRIED SUDDENLY THAT I SHOULD DRIVE RIGHT AWAY TO WATERLOO STATION WHERE HE PAID HIS FARE. THE GENTLEMAN TOLD ME HE WAS A DETECTIVE CALLED MR. SHERLOCK HOLMES, SIR.
HA! HA! HA! HA! EXCELLENT, WATSON! I SENSE A MIND AS QUICK AND SUPPLE AS MY OWN. SNAP GOES OUR SECOND THREAD, AND WE END WHERE WE BEGAN. THE CUNNING RASCAL!
THE FOLLOWING SATURDAY, HOLMES AND WATSON ARRIVE AT PADDINGTON STATION.
SEND ME REGULAR REPORTS AND WATCH BARRYMORE, STAPLETON, AND MR. FRANKLAND CAREFULLY. MORTIMER I BELIEVE IS ENTIRELY HONEST, BUT YOU MUST REPORT ALL.
I WILL DO MY BEST.
AND KEEP YOUR REVOLVER NEAR YOU NIGHT AND DAY - NEVER RELAX YOUR GUARD.
WATSON BIDS GOODBYE TO HOLMES AND JOINS MORTIMER AND SIR HENRY IN A FIRST-CLASS CARRIAGE.
I AM NOT TO LET YOU GO ABOUT ALONE, SIR HENRY. BY THE WAY, DID YOU FIND YOUR BLACK BOOT?
NO, IT IS GONE FOREVER.
THE JOURNEY TO DARTMOOR IS SWIFT AND PLEASANT. AS THE LANDSCAPE CHANGES FROM TOWERING BRICK TO WIDE VISTAS OF LUSH GRASS, SIR HENRY CRIES ALOUD WITH DELIGHT.
I HAVE SEEN MUCH OF THE WORLD SINCE I LEFT DEVON, DR. WATSON, BUT NO PLACE CAN COMPARE.

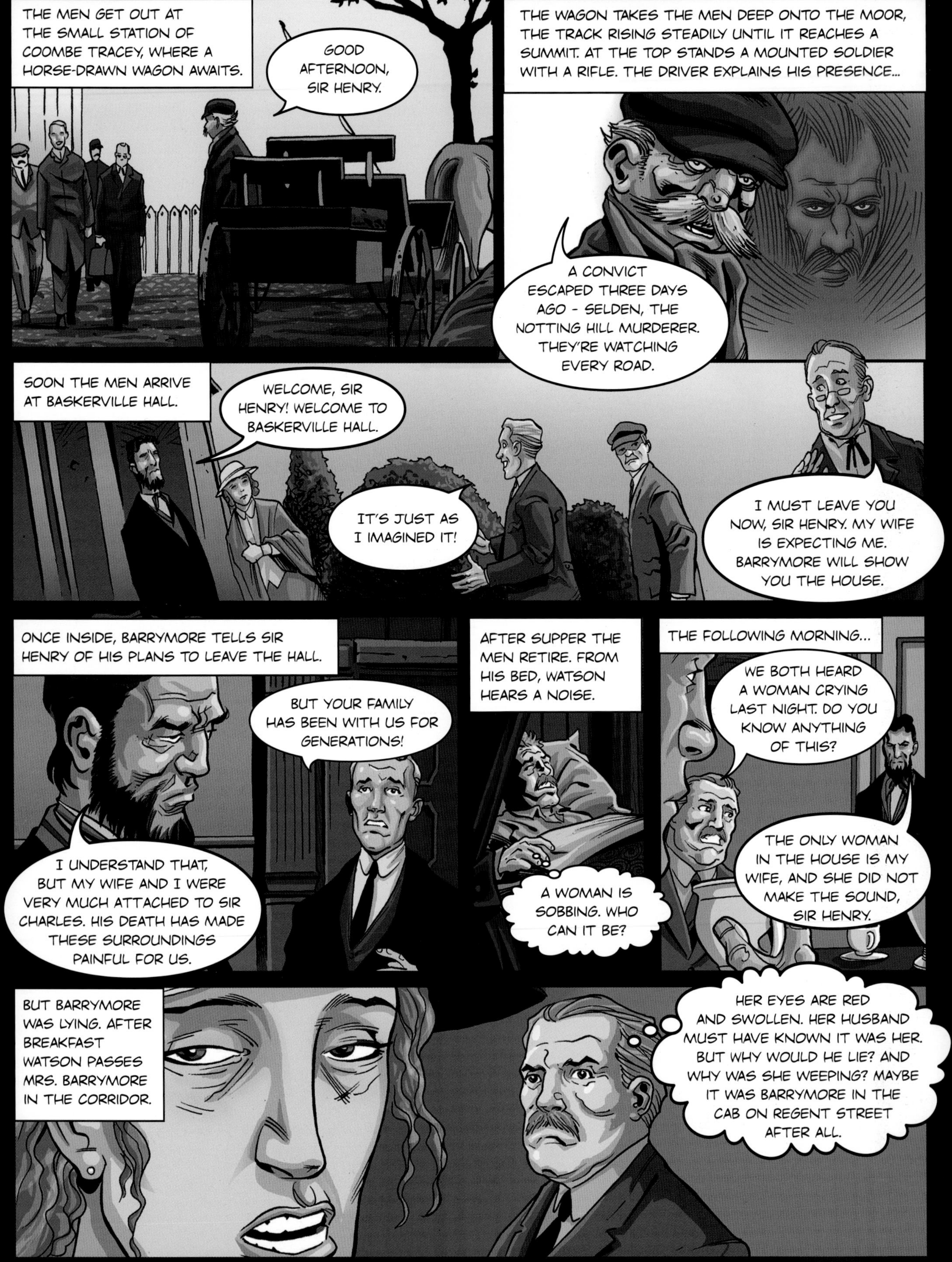

THE MEN GET OUT AT THE SMALL STATION OF COOMBE TRACEY, WHERE A HORSE-DRAWN WAGON AWAITS.
GOOD AFTERNOON, SIR HENRY.
THE WAGON TAKES THE MEN DEEP ONTO THE MOOR, THE TRACK RISING STEADILY UNTIL IT REACHES A SUMMIT. AT THE TOP STANDS A MOUNTED SOLDIER WITH A RIFLE. THE DRIVER EXPLAINS HIS PRESENCE...
A CONVICT ESCAPED THREE DAYS AGO - SELDEN, THE NOTTING HILL MURDERER. THEY'RE WATCHING EVERY ROAD.
SOON THE MEN ARRIVE AT BASKERVILLE HALL.
WELCOME, SIR HENRY! WELCOME TO BASKERVILLE HALL.
IT'S JUST AS I IMAGINED IT!
I MUST LEAVE YOU NOW, SIR HENRY. MY WIFE IS EXPECTING ME. BARRYMORE WILL SHOW YOU THE HOUSE.
ONCE INSIDE, BARRYMORE TELLS SIR HENRY OF HIS PLANS TO LEAVE THE HALL.
BUT YOUR FAMILY HAS BEEN WITH US FOR GENERATIONS!
I UNDERSTAND THAT, BUT MY WIFE AND I WERE VERY MUCH ATTACHED TO SIR CHARLES. HIS DEATH HAS MADE THESE SURROUNDINGS PAINFUL FOR US.
AFTER SUPPER THE MEN RETIRE. FROM HIS BED, WATSON HEARS A NOISE.
A WOMAN IS SOBBING. WHO CAN IT BE?
THE FOLLOWING MORNING...
WE BOTH HEARD A WOMAN CRYING LAST NIGHT. DO YOU KNOW ANYTHING OF THIS?
THE ONLY WOMAN IN THE HOUSE IS MY WIFE, AND SHE DID NOT MAKE THE SOUND, SIR HENRY.
BUT BARRYMORE WAS LYING. AFTER BREAKFAST WATSON PASSES MRS. BARRYMORE IN THE CORRIDOR.
HER EYES ARE RED AND SWOLLEN. HER HUSBAND MUST HAVE KNOWN IT WAS HER. BUT WHY WOULD HE LIE? AND WHY WAS SHE WEEPING? MAYBE IT WAS BARRYMORE IN THE CAB ON REGENT STREET AFTER ALL.

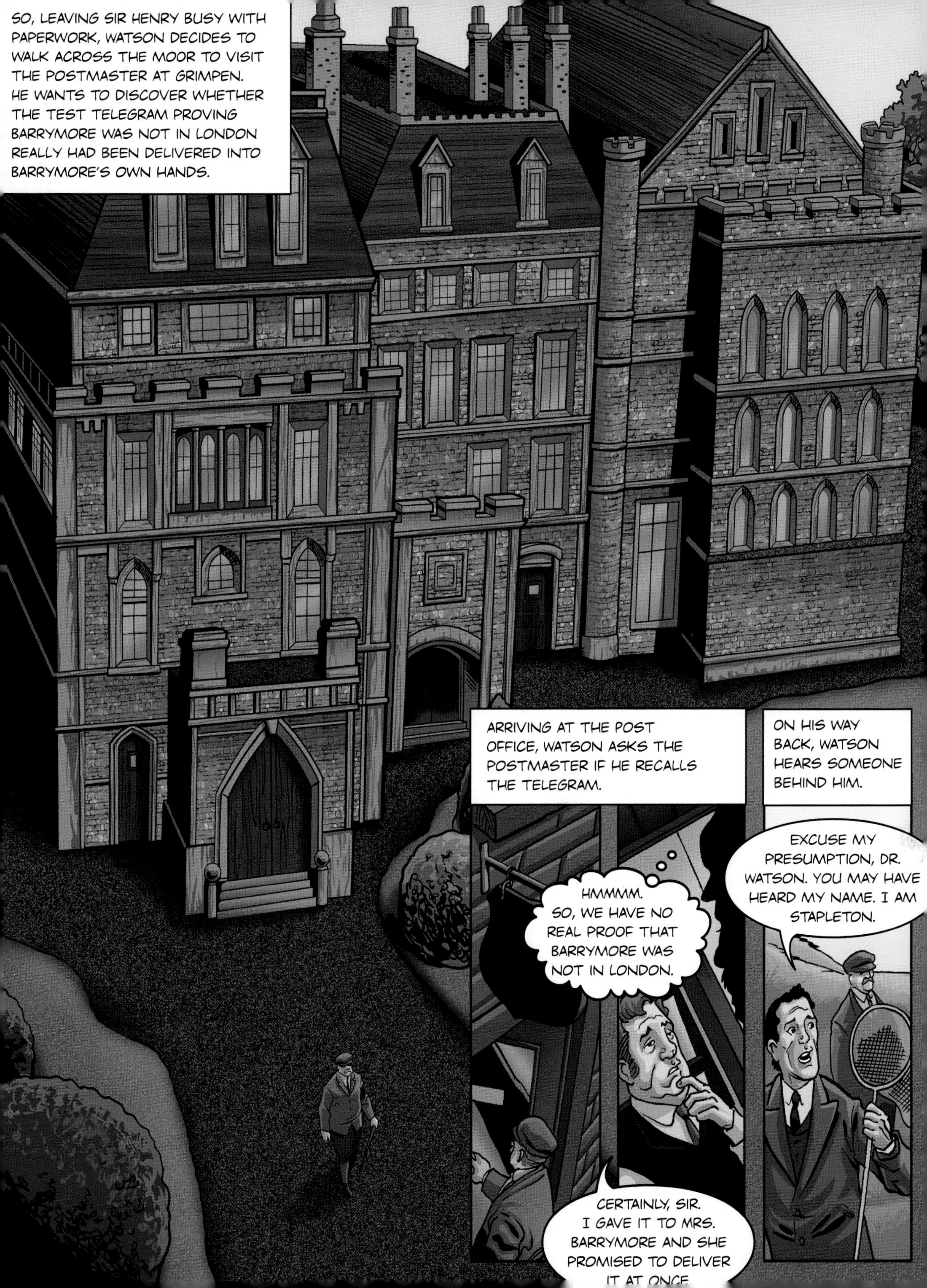
SO, LEAVING SIR HENRY BUSY WITH PAPERWORK, WATSON DECIDES TO WALK ACROSS THE MOOR TO VISIT THE POSTMASTER AT GRIMPEN. HE WANTS TO DISCOVER WHETHER THE TEST TELEGRAM PROVING BARRYMORE WAS NOT IN LONDON REALLY HAD BEEN DELIVERED INTO BARRYMORE'S OWN HANDS.
ARRIVING AT THE POST OFFICE, WATSON ASKS THE POSTMASTER IF HE RECALLS THE TELEGRAM.
HMMMM. SO, WE HAVE NO REAL PROOF THAT BARRYMORE WAS NOT IN LONDON.
CERTAINLY, SIR. I GAVE IT TO MRS. BARRYMORE AND SHE PROMISED TO DELIVER IT AT ONCE.
ON HIS WAY BACK, WATSON HEARS SOMEONE BEHIND HIM.
EXCUSE MY PRESUMPTION, DR. WATSON. YOU MAY HAVE HEARD MY NAME. I AM STAPLETON.

I TRUST THAT SIR HENRY IS NONE THE WORSE FOR HIS JOURNEY. WE WERE ALL RATHER AFRAID THAT AFTER THE SAD DEATH OF SIR CHARLES, HE MIGHT REFUSE TO LIVE HERE.
HE HAS NO SUPERSTITIOUS FEARS, I SUPPOSE? THE LEGEND OF THE HOUND TOOK SUCH A GREAT HOLD UPON THE IMAGINATION OF SIR CHARLES, I HAVE NO DOUBT IT LED TO HIS TRAGIC END.
BUT HOW?
I THINK HE REALLY DID SEE SOMETHING IN YEW ALLEY AND THAT THE SHOCK HAD A FATAL EFFECT UPON HIS DISEASED HEART. IT IS SUCH A SHAME. I WAS VERY FOND OF THE OLD MAN.
HOW DID YOU KNOW ABOUT HIS HEART?
MY FRIEND MORTIMER TOLD ME. AH, HERE IS MY HUMBLE ABODE - MERRIPIT HOUSE. I'D LIKE TO INTRODUCE YOU TO MY SISTER.
THAT WOULD BE NICE.
HOOOWWWWLLL...
WHAT WAS THAT?
THE PEASANTS SAY IT'S THE HOUND OF THE BASKERVILLES CALLING FOR ITS PREY. I THINK IT'S A POOR PONY THAT HAS WANDERED INTO THE MIRE AND HAS BEEN SUCKED DOWN. THE GREAT GRIMPEN MIRE IS A BAD PLACE. BUT I KNOW THE PATHS AROUND IT. AH, THERE IS MY SISTER...
OH, EXCUSE ME A MOMENT. IT'S A BUTTERFLY SELDOM SEEN IN THE LATE AUTUMN.

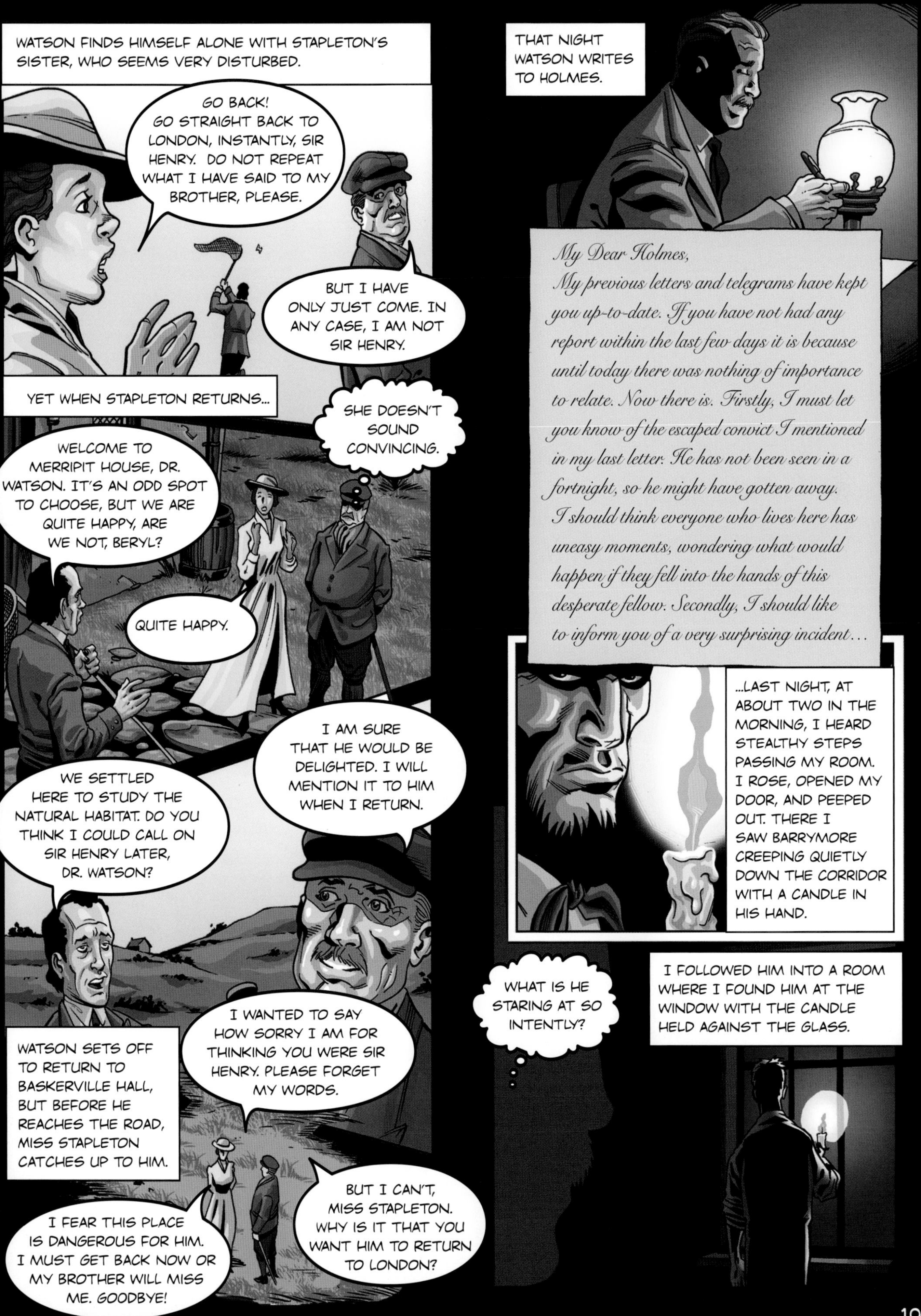
WATSON FINDS HIMSELF ALONE WITH STAPLETON'S SISTER, WHO SEEMS VERY DISTURBED.
GO BACK! GO STRAIGHT BACK TO LONDON, INSTANTLY, SIR HENRY. DO NOT REPEAT WHAT I HAVE SAID TO MY BROTHER, PLEASE.
BUT I HAVE ONLY JUST COME. IN ANY CASE, I AM NOT SIR HENRY.
YET WHEN STAPLETON RETURNS...
SHE DOESN'T SOUND CONVINCING.
WELCOME TO MERRIPIT HOUSE, DR. WATSON. IT'S AN ODD SPOT TO CHOOSE, BUT WE ARE QUITE HAPPY, ARE WE NOT, BERYL?
QUITE HAPPY.
WE SETTLED HERE TO STUDY THE NATURAL HABITAT. DO YOU THINK I COULD CALL ON SIR HENRY LATER, DR. WATSON?
I AM SURE THAT HE WOULD BE DELIGHTED. I WILL MENTION IT TO HIM WHEN I RETURN.
WATSON SETS OFF TO RETURN TO BASKERVILLE HALL, BUT BEFORE HE REACHES THE ROAD, MISS STAPLETON CATCHES UP TO HIM.
I WANTED TO SAY HOW SORRY I AM FOR THINKING YOU WERE SIR HENRY. PLEASE FORGET MY WORDS.
BUT I CAN'T, MISS STAPLETON. WHY IS IT THAT YOU WANT HIM TO RETURN TO LONDON?
I FEAR THIS PLACE IS DANGEROUS FOR HIM. I MUST GET BACK NOW OR MY BROTHER WILL MISS ME. GOODBYE!
THAT NIGHT WATSON WRITES TO HOLMES.
My Dear Holmes,
My previous letters and telegrams have kept you up-to-date. If you have not had any report within the last few days it is because until today there was nothing of importance to relate. Now there is. Firstly, I must let you know of the escaped convict I mentioned in my last letter. He has not been seen in a fortnight, so he might have gotten away. I should think everyone who lives here has uneasy moments, wondering what would happen if they fell into the hands of this desperate fellow. Secondly, I should like to inform you of a very surprising incident…
...LAST NIGHT, AT ABOUT TWO IN THE MORNING, I HEARD STEALTHY STEPS PASSING MY ROOM. I ROSE, OPENED MY DOOR, AND PEEPED OUT. THERE I SAW BARRYMORE CREEPING QUIETLY DOWN THE CORRIDOR WITH A CANDLE IN HIS HAND.
WHAT IS HE STARING AT SO INTENTLY?
I FOLLOWED HIM INTO A ROOM WHERE I FOUND HIM AT THE WINDOW WITH THE CANDLE HELD AGAINST THE GLASS.

My Dear Holmes,
If my news was sparse in the early days of our mission, you must acknowledge that events are now occurring thick and fast. In my last report, I ended with Barrymore at the window and now, 48 hours later, events have taken a turn I could not have anticipated. Before breakfast on the morning following my adventure, I returned to examine the room in which Barrymore had been the night before. I noticed that the window commands the nearest outlook over the moor...
SO BARRYMORE MUST HAVE BEEN LOOKING OUT FOR SOMETHING OR SOMEONE ON THE MOOR.
I TOLD SIR HENRY AND HE SUGGESTED THAT WE SHADOW BARRYMORE THAT NIGHT TO TRY TO SEE WHAT HE WAS UP TO.
WHAT IF HE HEARS US?
HE IS RATHER DEAF AND ANYWAY, WE MUST TAKE OUR CHANCES.
NIGHT FELL AND WE FOLLOWED BARRYMORE AGAIN. THIS TIME, AS HE STOOD AT THE WINDOW, SIR HENRY ADDRESSED HIM DIRECTLY.
WHAT ARE YOU UP TO BARRYMORE?
DON'T ASK ME, SIR HENRY - DON'T ASK ME. I GIVE YOU MY WORD THAT IT IS NOT MY SECRET AND THAT I CANNOT TELL IT.
A SUDDEN IDEA OCCURRED TO ME AND I HELD THE CANDLE AT THE WINDOW.
HE MUST HAVE BEEN HOLDING IT AS A SIGNAL.
SEE, THERE IS A LIGHT OUTSIDE THAT MOVES ALSO. WHO IS IT, MAN?
BARRYMORE WOULD SAY NOTHING. THEN MRS. BARRYMORE SPOKE.
MY BROTHER, IS THE ESCAPED CONVICT. THE LIGHT IS A SIGNAL THAT FOOD IS READY FOR HIM TO COLLECT.
WITHOUT DELAY, SIR HENRY AND I TOOK TO THE MOOR.
I HAVE MY REVOLVER. AND YOU?
ARE YOU ARMED?
A HUNTING WHIP. WE SHALL TAKE HIM BY SURPRISE AND HAVE HIM AT OUR MERCY.

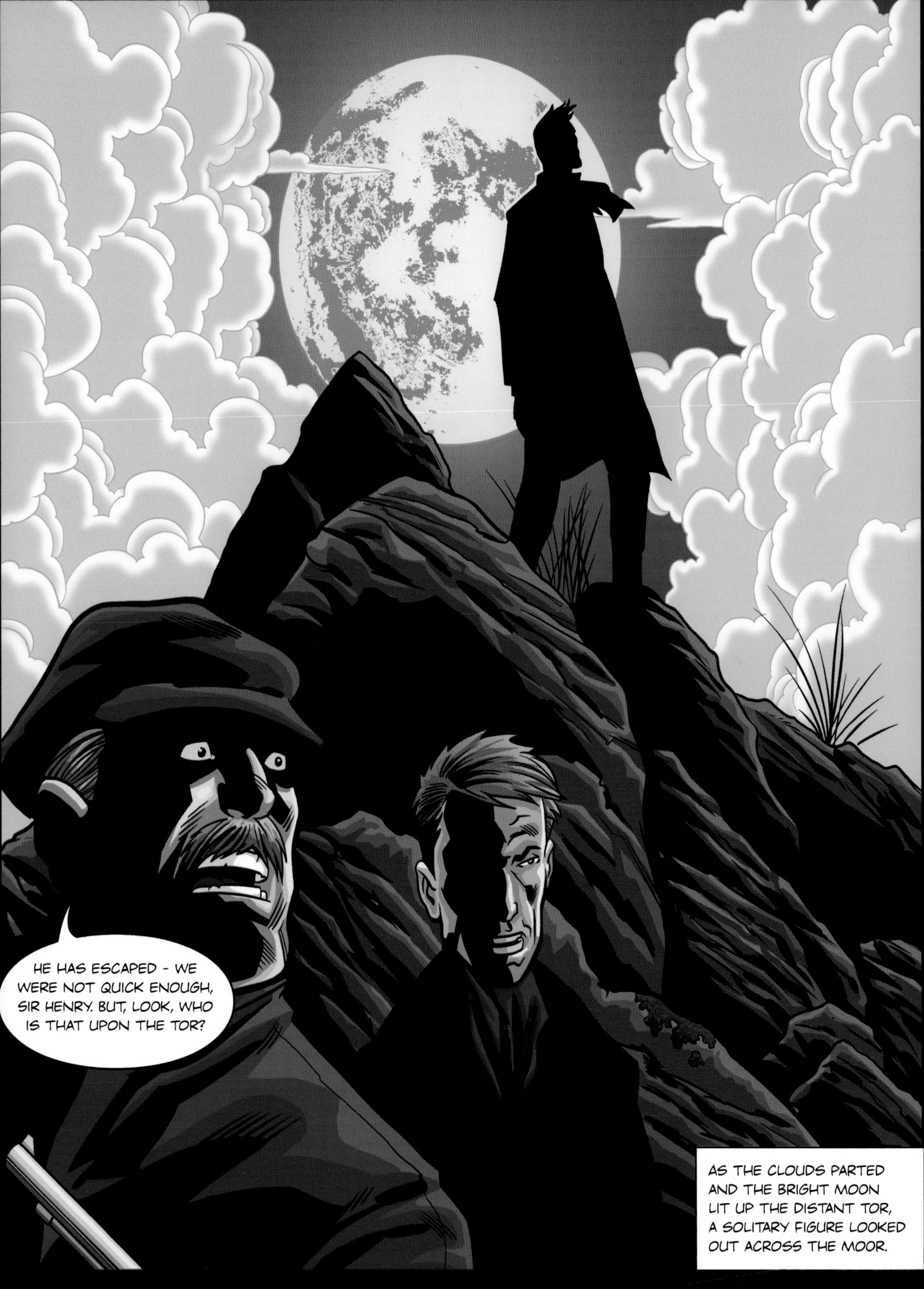
HE HAS ESCAPED - WE WERE NOT QUICK ENOUGH, SIR HENRY. BUT, LOOK, WHO IS THAT UPON THE TOR?
AS THE CLOUDS PARTED AND THE BRIGHT MOON LIT UP THE DISTANT TOR, A SOLITARY FIGURE LOOKED OUT ACROSS THE MOOR.

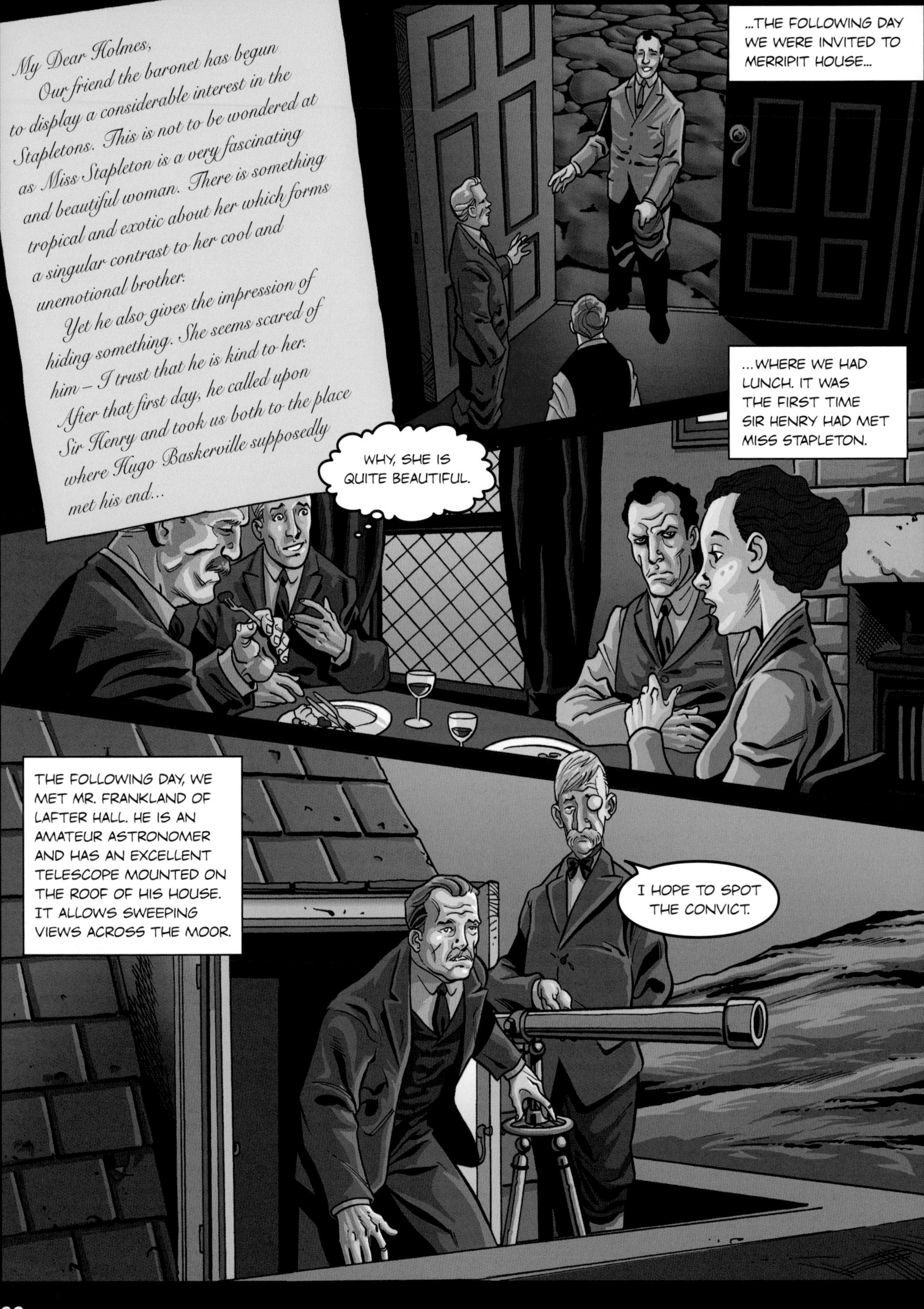
My Dear Holmes,
Our friend the baronet has begun to display a considerable interest in the Stapletons. This is not to be wondered at as Miss Stapleton is a very fascinating and beautiful woman. There is something tropical and exotic about her which forms a singular contrast to her cool and unemotional brother.
Yet he also gives the impression of hiding something. She seems scared of him – I trust that he is kind to her.
After that first day, he called upon Sir Henry and took us both to the place where Hugo Baskerville supposedly met his end...
...THE FOLLOWING DAY WE WERE INVITED TO MERRIPIT HOUSE...
...WHERE WE HAD LUNCH. IT WAS THE FIRST TIME SIR HENRY HAD MET MISS STAPLETON.
WHY, SHE IS QUITE BEAUTIFUL.
THE FOLLOWING DAY, WE MET MR. FRANKLAND OF LAFTER HALL. HE IS AN AMATEUR ASTRONOMER AND HAS AN EXCELLENT TELESCOPE MOUNTED ON THE ROOF OF HIS HOUSE. IT ALLOWS SWEEPING VIEWS ACROSS THE MOOR.
I HOPE TO SPOT THE CONVICT.

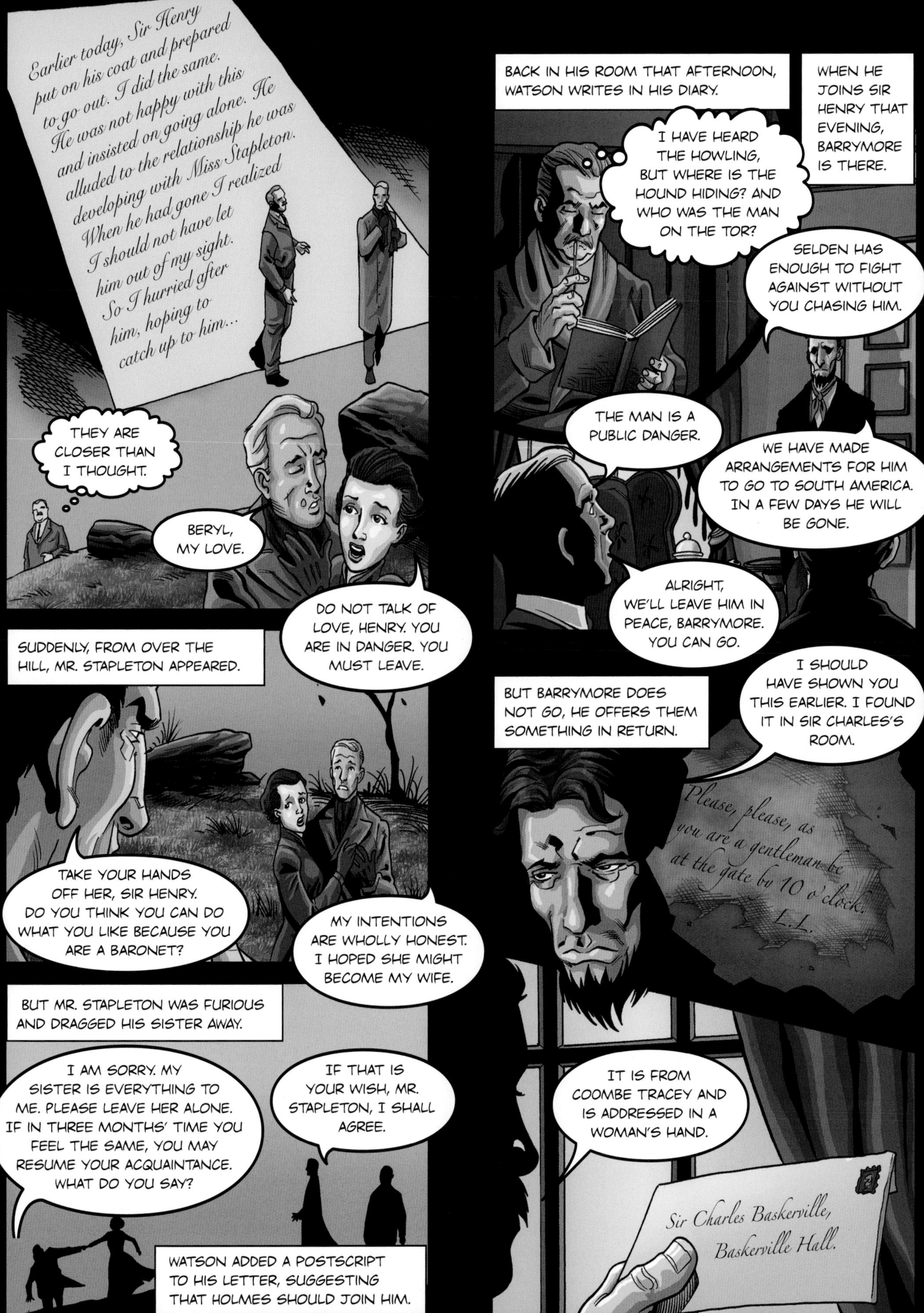
Earlier today, Sir Henry put on his coat and prepared to go out. I did the same. He was not happy with this and insisted on going alone. He alluded to the relationship he was developing with Miss Stapleton. When he had gone I realized I should not have let him out of my sight. So I hurried after him, hoping to catch up to him...
THEY ARE CLOSER THAN I THOUGHT.
BERYL, MY LOVE.
DO NOT TALK OF LOVE, HENRY. YOU ARE IN DANGER. YOU MUST LEAVE.
SUDDENLY, FROM OVER THE HILL, MR. STAPLETON APPEARED.
TAKE YOUR HANDS OFF HER, SIR HENRY. DO YOU THINK YOU CAN DO WHAT YOU LIKE BECAUSE YOU ARE A BARONET?
MY INTENTIONS ARE WHOLLY HONEST. I HOPED SHE MIGHT BECOME MY WIFE.
BUT MR. STAPLETON WAS FURIOUS AND DRAGGED HIS SISTER AWAY.
I AM SORRY. MY SISTER IS EVERYTHING TO ME. PLEASE LEAVE HER ALONE. IF IN THREE MONTHS' TIME YOU FEEL THE SAME, YOU MAY RESUME YOUR ACQUAINTANCE. WHAT DO YOU SAY?
IF THAT IS YOUR WISH, MR. STAPLETON, I SHALL AGREE.
WATSON ADDED A POSTSCRIPT TO HIS LETTER, SUGGESTING THAT HOLMES SHOULD JOIN HIM.
BACK IN HIS ROOM THAT AFTERNOON, WATSON WRITES IN HIS DIARY.
I HAVE HEARD THE HOWLING, BUT WHERE IS THE HOUND HIDING? AND WHO WAS THE MAN ON THE TOR?
WHEN HE JOINS SIR HENRY THAT EVENING, BARRYMORE IS THERE.
SELDEN HAS ENOUGH TO FIGHT AGAINST WITHOUT YOU CHASING HIM.
THE MAN IS A PUBLIC DANGER.
WE HAVE MADE ARRANGEMENTS FOR HIM TO GO TO SOUTH AMERICA. IN A FEW DAYS HE WILL BE GONE.
ALRIGHT, WE'LL LEAVE HIM IN PEACE, BARRYMORE. YOU CAN GO.
BUT BARRYMORE DOES NOT GO, HE OFFERS THEM SOMETHING IN RETURN.
I SHOULD HAVE SHOWN YOU THIS EARLIER. I FOUND IT IN SIR CHARLES'S ROOM.
Please, please, as you are a gentleman be at the gate by 10 o'clock. L.L.
IT IS FROM COOMBE TRACEY AND IS ADDRESSED IN A WOMAN'S HAND.
Sir Charles Baskerville, Baskerville Hall.

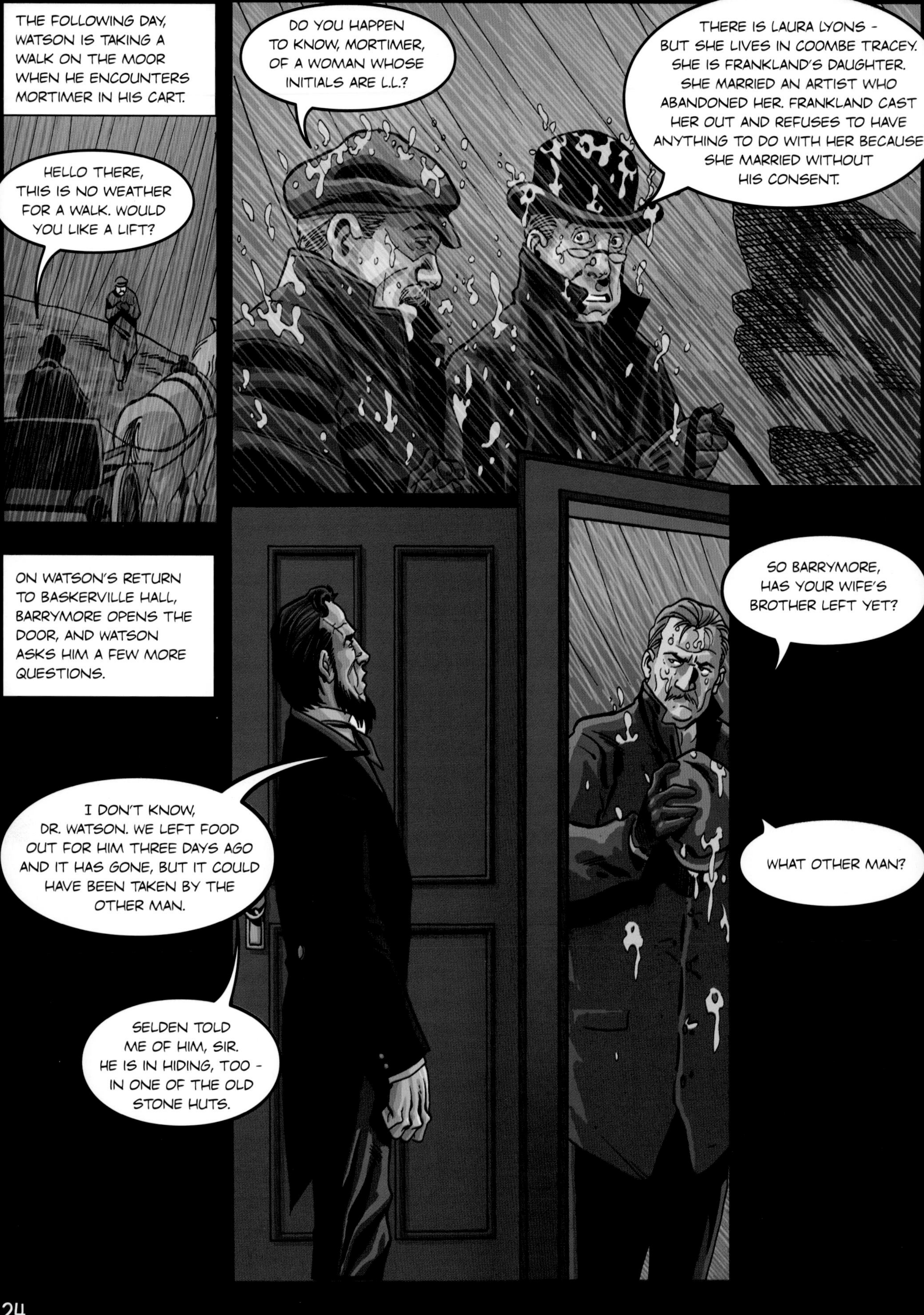
THE FOLLOWING DAY, WATSON IS TAKING A WALK ON THE MOOR WHEN HE ENCOUNTERS MORTIMER IN HIS CART.
HELLO THERE, THIS IS NO WEATHER FOR A WALK. WOULD YOU LIKE A LIFT?
DO YOU HAPPEN TO KNOW, MORTIMER, OF A WOMAN WHOSE INITIALS ARE L.L.?
THERE IS LAURA LYONS - BUT SHE LIVES IN COOMBE TRACEY. SHE IS FRANKLAND'S DAUGHTER. SHE MARRIED AN ARTIST WHO ABANDONED HER. FRANKLAND CAST HER OUT AND REFUSES TO HAVE ANYTHING TO DO WITH HER BECAUSE SHE MARRIED WITHOUT HIS CONSENT.
ON WATSON'S RETURN TO BASKERVILLE HALL, BARRYMORE OPENS THE DOOR, AND WATSON ASKS HIM A FEW MORE QUESTIONS.
SO BARRYMORE, HAS YOUR WIFE'S BROTHER LEFT YET?
I DON'T KNOW, DR. WATSON. WE LEFT FOOD OUT FOR HIM THREE DAYS AGO AND IT HAS GONE, BUT IT COULD HAVE BEEN TAKEN BY THE OTHER MAN.
WHAT OTHER MAN?
SELDEN TOLD ME OF HIM, SIR. HE IS IN HIDING, TOO - IN ONE OF THE OLD STONE HUTS.

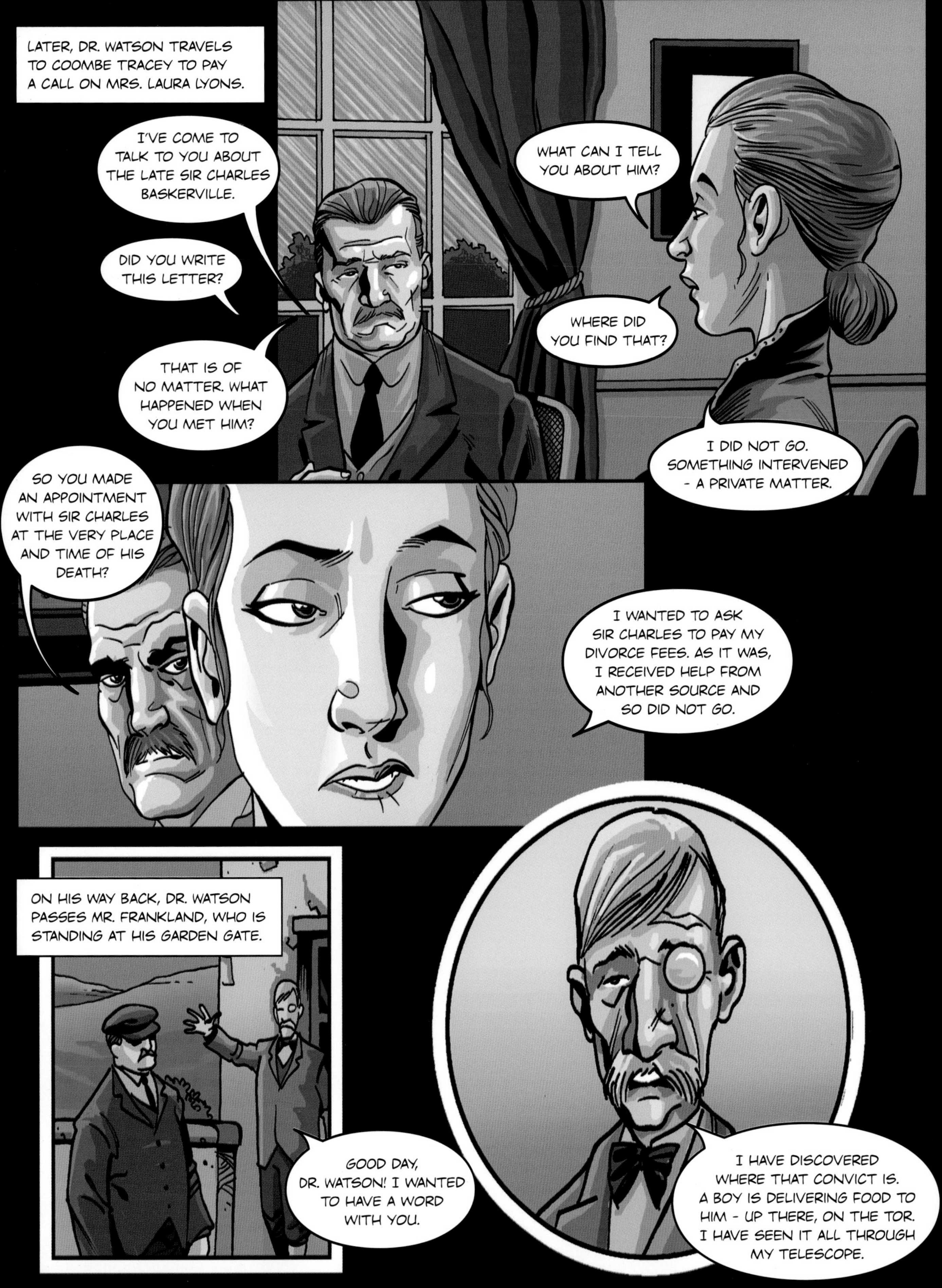
LATER, DR. WATSON TRAVELS TO COOMBE TRACEY TO PAY A CALL ON MRS. LAURA LYONS.
I'VE COME TO TALK TO YOU ABOUT THE LATE SIR CHARLES BASKERVILLE.
WHAT CAN I TELL YOU ABOUT HIM?
DID YOU WRITE THIS LETTER?
WHERE DID YOU FIND THAT?
THAT IS OF NO MATTER. WHAT HAPPENED WHEN YOU MET HIM?
I DID NOT GO. SOMETHING INTERVENED - A PRIVATE MATTER.
SO YOU MADE AN APPOINTMENT WITH SIR CHARLES AT THE VERY PLACE AND TIME OF HIS DEATH?
I WANTED TO ASK SIR CHARLES TO PAY MY DIVORCE FEES. AS IT WAS, I RECEIVED HELP FROM ANOTHER SOURCE AND SO DID NOT GO.
ON HIS WAY BACK, DR. WATSON PASSES MR. FRANKLAND, WHO IS STANDING AT HIS GARDEN GATE.
GOOD DAY, DR. WATSON! I WANTED TO HAVE A WORD WITH YOU.
I HAVE DISCOVERED WHERE THAT CONVICT IS. A BOY IS DELIVERING FOOD TO HIM - UP THERE, ON THE TOR. I HAVE SEEN IT ALL THROUGH MY TELESCOPE.

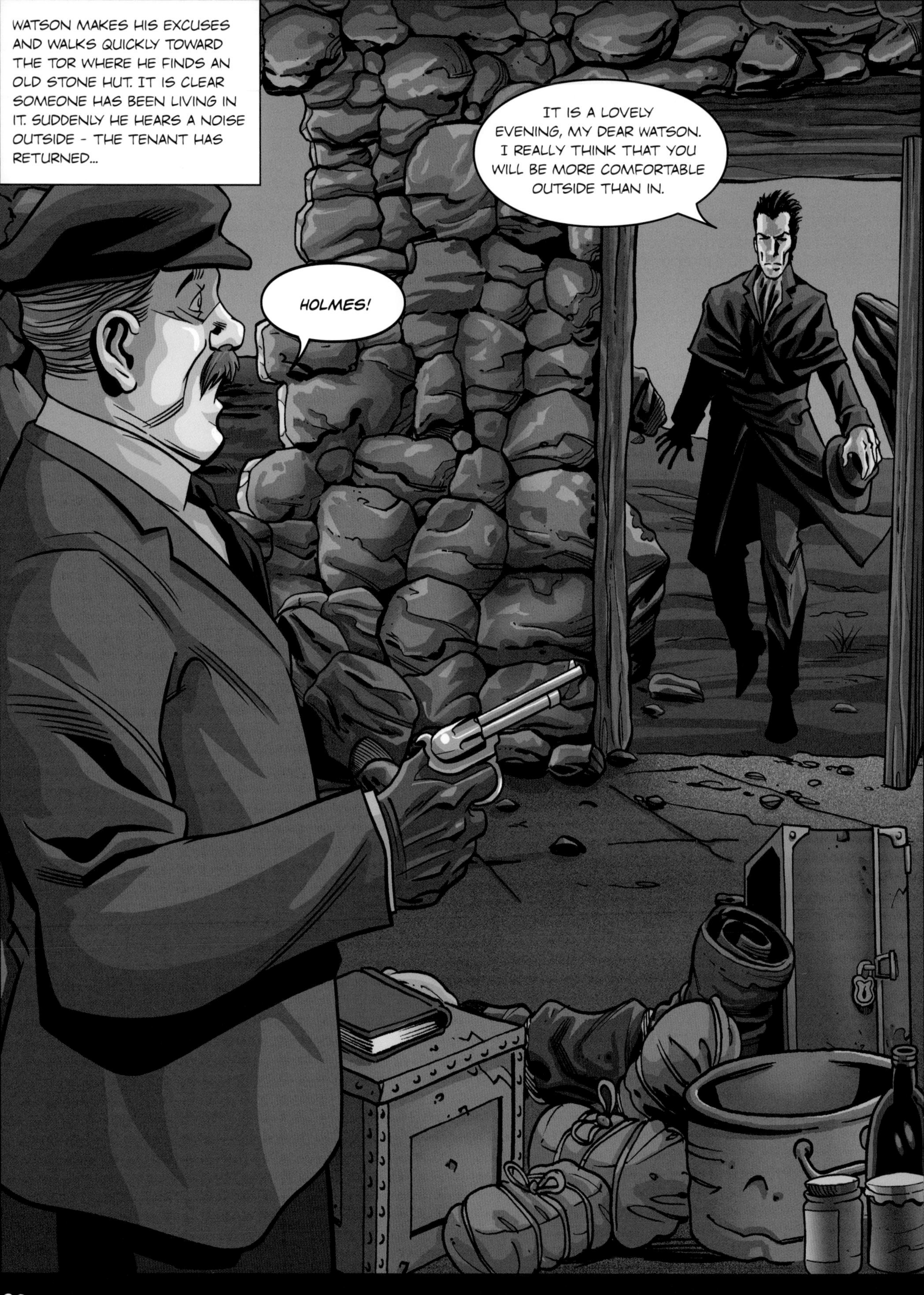
WATSON MAKES HIS EXCUSES AND WALKS QUICKLY TOWARD THE TOR WHERE HE FINDS AN OLD STONE HUT. IT IS CLEAR SOMEONE HAS BEEN LIVING IN IT. SUDDENLY HE HEARS A NOISE OUTSIDE - THE TENANT HAS RETURNED...
IT IS A LOVELY EVENING, MY DEAR WATSON. I REALLY THINK THAT YOU WILL BE MORE COMFORTABLE OUTSIDE THAN IN.
HOLMES!

I CAME A WEEK AGO. A LOCAL BOY HAS BEEN RUNNING MY ERRANDS.
I AM GLAD THAT YOU ARE HERE, HOLMES, BUT WHY NOT TELL ME? DON'T YOU TRUST ME?
MY PRESENCE WOULD HAVE WARNED OUR OPPONENTS. IT WAS BETTER THAT NO ONE KNEW. BUT WHAT ABOUT LAURA LYONS? YOU KNOW THERE IS A CLOSE INTIMACY BETWEEN HER AND STAPLETON?
STAPLETON?
YES, AND THE WOMAN HE CALLS HIS SISTER IS IN FACT HIS WIFE! HE IS OUR MURDERER AND SIR HENRY IS HIS NEXT VICTIM. I AM CERTAIN OF IT.
EEEEEEEE OOOOWWW!!
GRRRRRRR!!
THE HOUND! COME, WATSON, LET US HOPE WE ARE NOT TOO LATE.
AS THE TWO MEN RUN SWIFTLY ACROSS THE MOOR, THEY HEAR A LAST DESPAIRING YELL, THEN A DULL, HEAVY THUD.
HE HAS BEATEN US, WATSON, WE ARE TOO LATE! LOOK, IT IS SIR HENRY. I RECOGNIZE HIS TWEED SUIT.
NO! I SHOULD NEVER HAVE ABANDONED HIM THIS AFTERNOON.
ON THE ROCKS AHEAD IS A BODY FACEDOWN ON THE GROUND. HOLMES REACHES IT FIRST AND, PUTTING A HAND ON ITS SHOULDER, TURNS THE BODY OVER.
BUT THIS IS NOT THE BARONET. IT IS SELDEN, THE CONVICT, WEARING SIR HENRY'S CLOTHES. THEY HAVE BEEN THE POOR FELLOW'S DEATH. THE HOUND HAD THE SCENT FROM SIR HENRY'S BOOT AND TRACKED HIM DOWN.
WHAT IS THIS? IS SOMEBODY HURT?
SUDDENLY, STAPLETON APPEARS FROM ACROSS THE MOOR.

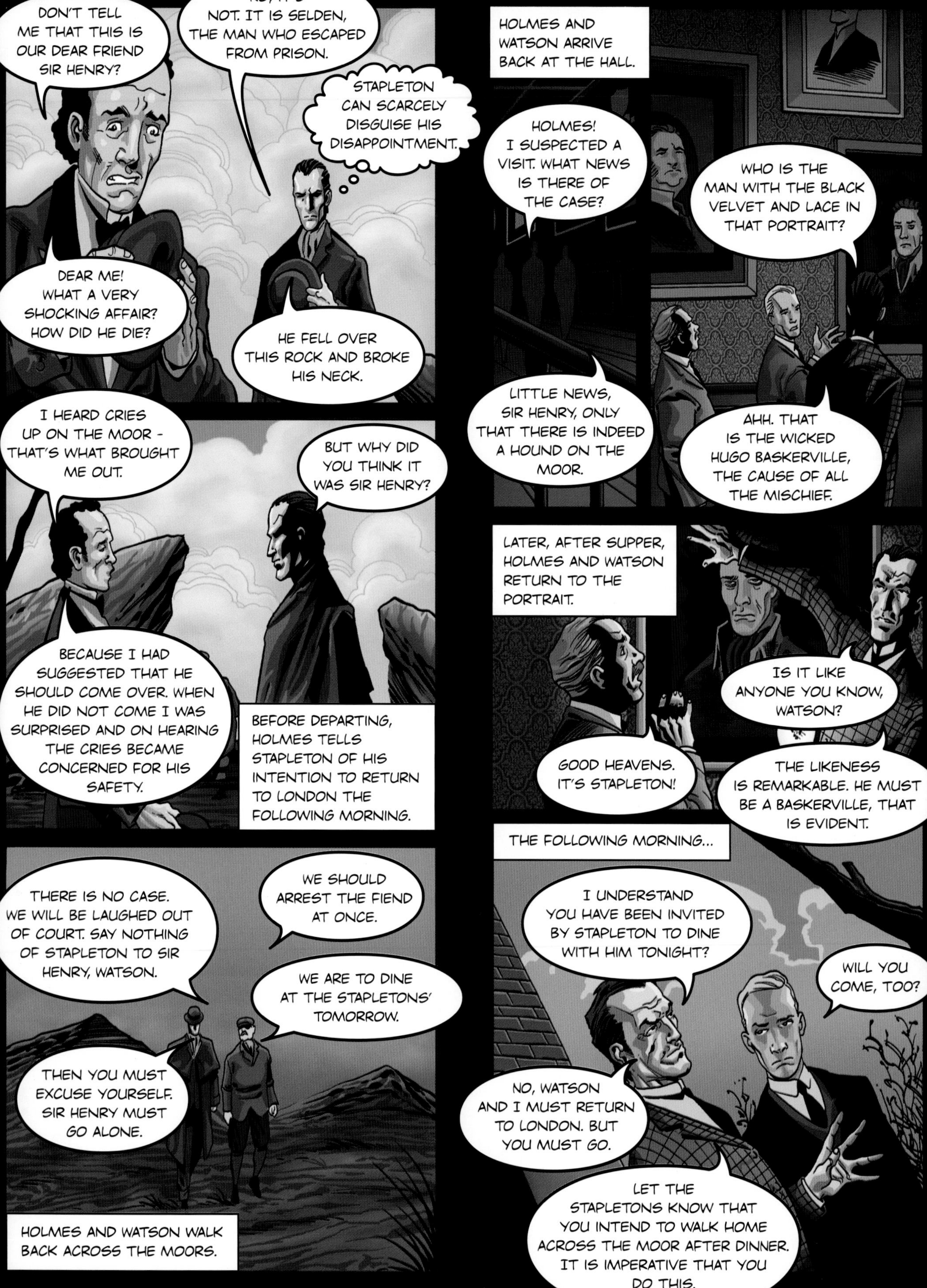
DON'T TELL ME THAT THIS IS OUR DEAR FRIEND SIR HENRY?
NO, IT'S NOT. IT IS SELDEN, THE MAN WHO ESCAPED FROM PRISON.
STAPLETON CAN SCARCELY DISGUISE HIS DISAPPOINTMENT.
DEAR ME! WHAT A VERY SHOCKING AFFAIR? HOW DID HE DIE?
HE FELL OVER THIS ROCK AND BROKE HIS NECK.
I HEARD CRIES UP ON THE MOOR - THAT'S WHAT BROUGHT ME OUT.
BUT WHY DID YOU THINK IT WAS SIR HENRY?
BECAUSE I HAD SUGGESTED THAT HE SHOULD COME OVER. WHEN HE DID NOT COME I WAS SURPRISED AND ON HEARING THE CRIES BECAME CONCERNED FOR HIS SAFETY.
BEFORE DEPARTING, HOLMES TELLS STAPLETON OF HIS INTENTION TO RETURN TO LONDON THE FOLLOWING MORNING.
THERE IS NO CASE. WE WILL BE LAUGHED OUT OF COURT. SAY NOTHING OF STAPLETON TO SIR HENRY, WATSON.
WE SHOULD ARREST THE FIEND AT ONCE.
WE ARE TO DINE AT THE STAPLETONS' TOMORROW.
THEN YOU MUST EXCUSE YOURSELF. SIR HENRY MUST GO ALONE.
HOLMES AND WATSON WALK BACK ACROSS THE MOORS.
HOLMES AND WATSON ARRIVE BACK AT THE HALL.
HOLMES! I SUSPECTED A VISIT. WHAT NEWS IS THERE OF THE CASE?
WHO IS THE MAN WITH THE BLACK VELVET AND LACE IN THAT PORTRAIT?
LITTLE NEWS, SIR HENRY, ONLY THAT THERE IS INDEED A HOUND ON THE MOOR.
AHH. THAT IS THE WICKED HUGO BASKERVILLE, THE CAUSE OF ALL THE MISCHIEF.
LATER, AFTER SUPPER, HOLMES AND WATSON RETURN TO THE PORTRAIT.
IS IT LIKE ANYONE YOU KNOW, WATSON?
GOOD HEAVENS. IT'S STAPLETON!
THE LIKENESS IS REMARKABLE. HE MUST BE A BASKERVILLE, THAT IS EVIDENT.
THE FOLLOWING MORNING...
I UNDERSTAND YOU HAVE BEEN INVITED BY STAPLETON TO DINE WITH HIM TONIGHT?
WILL YOU COME, TOO?
NO, WATSON AND I MUST RETURN TO LONDON. BUT YOU MUST GO.
LET THE STAPLETONS KNOW THAT YOU INTEND TO WALK HOME ACROSS THE MOOR AFTER DINNER. IT IS IMPERATIVE THAT YOU DO THIS.

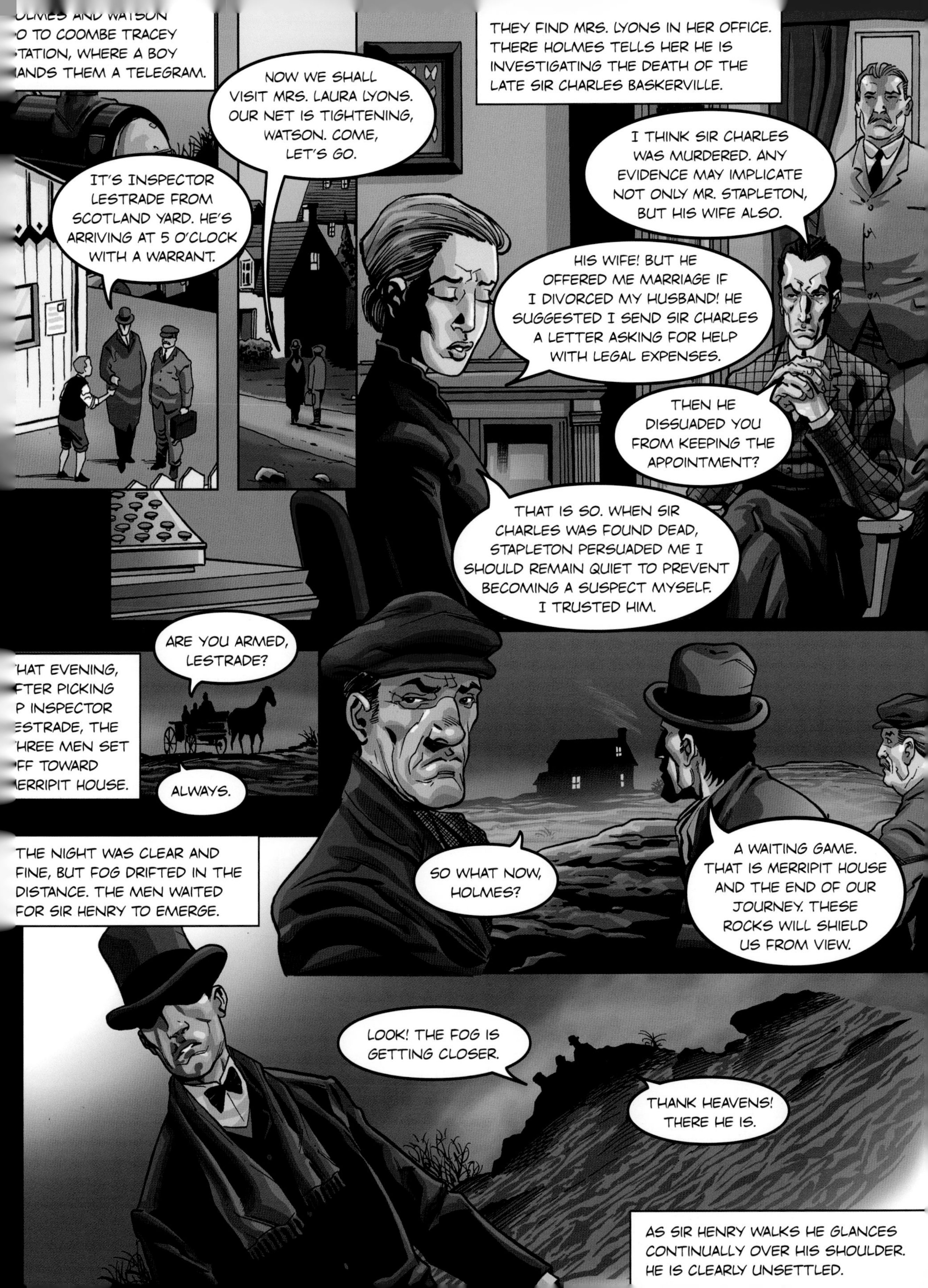

OLMES AND WATSON
O TO COOMBE TRACEY
TATION, WHERE A BOY
ANDS THEM A TELEGRAM.
IT'S INSPECTOR LESTRADE FROM SCOTLAND YARD. HE'S ARRIVING AT 5 O'CLOCK WITH A WARRANT.
NOW WE SHALL VISIT MRS. LAURA LYONS. OUR NET IS TIGHTENING, WATSON. COME, LET'S GO.
THEY FIND MRS. LYONS IN HER OFFICE. THERE HOLMES TELLS HER HE IS INVESTIGATING THE DEATH OF THE LATE SIR CHARLES BASKERVILLE.
I THINK SIR CHARLES WAS MURDERED. ANY EVIDENCE MAY IMPLICATE NOT ONLY MR. STAPLETON, BUT HIS WIFE ALSO.
HIS WIFE! BUT HE OFFERED ME MARRIAGE IF I DIVORCED MY HUSBAND! HE SUGGESTED I SEND SIR CHARLES A LETTER ASKING FOR HELP WITH LEGAL EXPENSES.
THEN HE DISSUADED YOU FROM KEEPING THE APPOINTMENT?
THAT IS SO. WHEN SIR CHARLES WAS FOUND DEAD, STAPLETON PERSUADED ME I SHOULD REMAIN QUIET TO PREVENT BECOMING A SUSPECT MYSELF. I TRUSTED HIM.
HAT EVENING, FTER PICKING P INSPECTOR ESTRADE, THE HREE MEN SET FF TOWARD ERRIPIT HOUSE.
ARE YOU ARMED, LESTRADE?
ALWAYS.
THE NIGHT WAS CLEAR AND FINE, BUT FOG DRIFTED IN THE DISTANCE. THE MEN WAITED FOR SIR HENRY TO EMERGE.
SO WHAT NOW, HOLMES?
A WAITING GAME. THAT IS MERRIPIT HOUSE AND THE END OF OUR JOURNEY. THESE ROCKS WILL SHIELD US FROM VIEW.
LOOK! THE FOG IS GETTING CLOSER.
THANK HEAVENS! THERE HE IS.
AS SIR HENRY WALKS HE GLANCES CONTINUALLY OVER HIS SHOULDER. HE IS CLEARLY UNSETTLED.

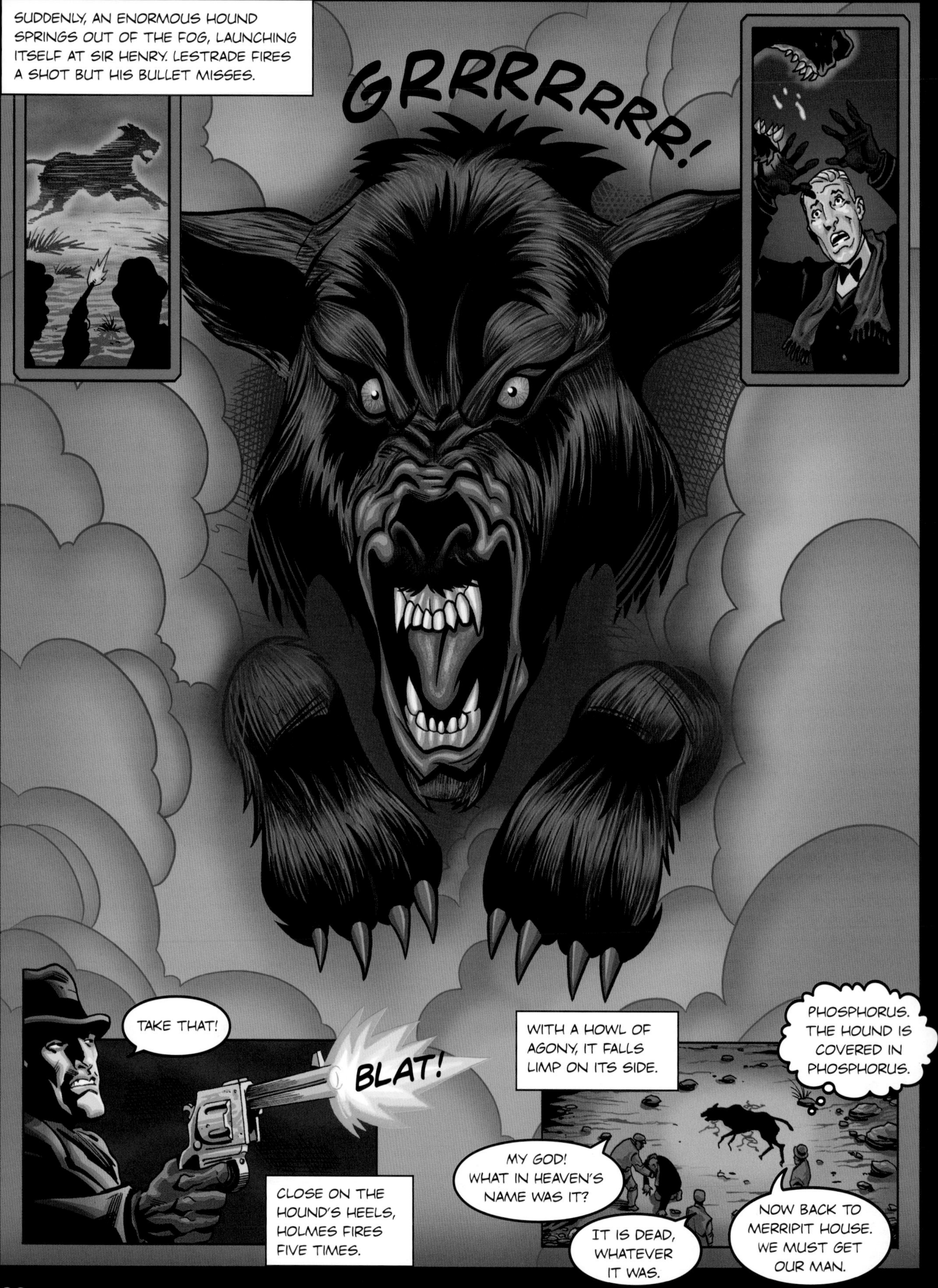
SUDDENLY, AN ENORMOUS HOUND SPRINGS OUT OF THE FOG, LAUNCHING ITSELF AT SIR HENRY. LESTRADE FIRES A SHOT BUT HIS BULLET MISSES.
GRRRRRRR!
TAKE THAT!
BLAT!
CLOSE ON THE HOUND'S HEELS, HOLMES FIRES FIVE TIMES.
WITH A HOWL OF AGONY, IT FALLS LIMP ON ITS SIDE.
PHOSPHORUS. THE HOUND IS COVERED IN PHOSPHORUS.
MY GOD! WHAT IN HEAVEN'S NAME WAS IT?
IT IS DEAD, WHATEVER IT WAS.
NOW BACK TO MERRIPIT HOUSE. WE MUST GET OUR MAN.

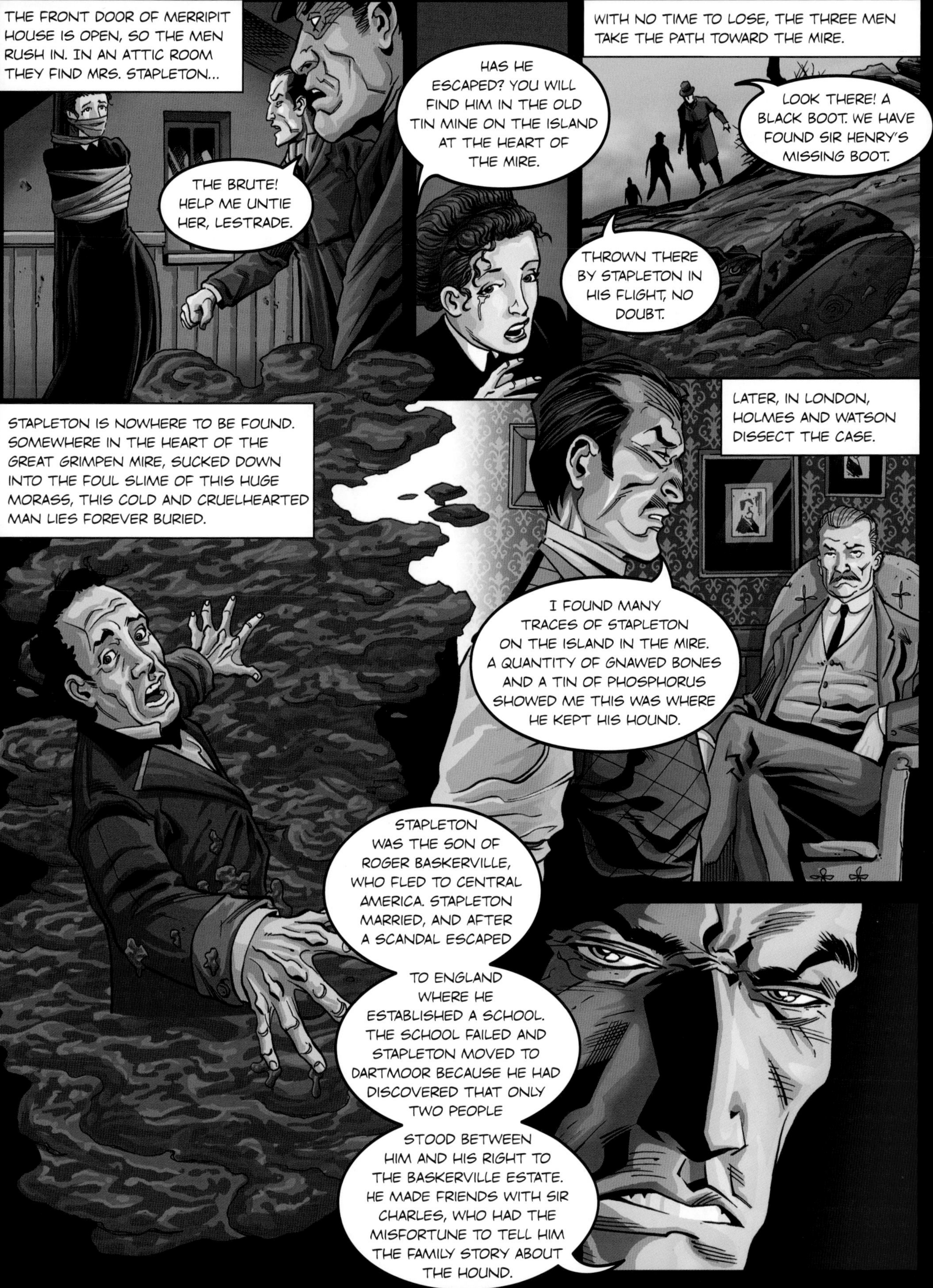
THE FRONT DOOR OF MERRIPIT HOUSE IS OPEN, SO THE MEN RUSH IN. IN AN ATTIC ROOM THEY FIND MRS. STAPLETON...
THE BRUTE! HELP ME UNTIE HER, LESTRADE.
HAS HE ESCAPED? YOU WILL FIND HIM IN THE OLD TIN MINE ON THE ISLAND AT THE HEART OF THE MIRE.
WITH NO TIME TO LOSE, THE THREE MEN TAKE THE PATH TOWARD THE MIRE.
LOOK THERE! A BLACK BOOT. WE HAVE FOUND SIR HENRY'S MISSING BOOT.
THROWN THERE BY STAPLETON IN HIS FLIGHT, NO DOUBT.
STAPLETON IS NOWHERE TO BE FOUND. SOMEWHERE IN THE HEART OF THE GREAT GRIMPEN MIRE, SUCKED DOWN INTO THE FOUL SLIME OF THIS HUGE MORASS, THIS COLD AND CRUELHEARTED MAN LIES FOREVER BURIED.
LATER, IN LONDON, HOLMES AND WATSON DISSECT THE CASE.
I FOUND MANY TRACES OF STAPLETON ON THE ISLAND IN THE MIRE. A QUANTITY OF GNAWED BONES AND A TIN OF PHOSPHORUS SHOWED ME THIS WAS WHERE HE KEPT HIS HOUND.
STAPLETON WAS THE SON OF ROGER BASKERVILLE, WHO FLED TO CENTRAL AMERICA. STAPLETON MARRIED, AND AFTER A SCANDAL ESCAPED
TO ENGLAND WHERE HE ESTABLISHED A SCHOOL. THE SCHOOL FAILED AND STAPLETON MOVED TO DARTMOOR BECAUSE HE HAD DISCOVERED THAT ONLY TWO PEOPLE
STOOD BETWEEN HIM AND HIS RIGHT TO THE BASKERVILLE ESTATE. HE MADE FRIENDS WITH SIR CHARLES, WHO HAD THE MISFORTUNE TO TELL HIM THE FAMILY STORY ABOUT THE HOUND.

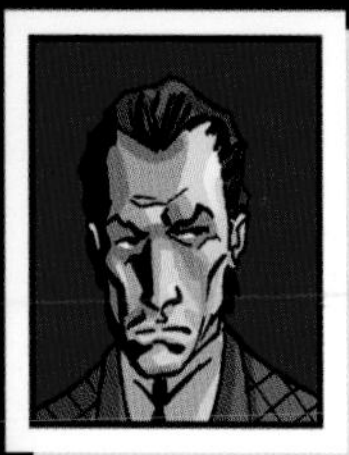

IN PRESENTING HIS WIFE AS HIS SISTER, HE WAS ABLE TO CULTIVATE A FRIENDSHIP WITH LAURA LYONS. THIS, IN TURN, ENABLED HIM TO LURE SIR CHARLES CLOSE ENOUGH TO THE MOOR GATE FOR THE HOUND TO STARTLE HIM. HAVING LEARNED FROM MORTIMER THAT SIR CHARLES HAD A WEAK HEART, STAPLETON PLANNED HIS DEATH - OF THAT I HAVE NO DOUBT. STAPLETON'S ONLY ACCOMPLICE, HIS WIFE, COULD NEVER GIVE HIM AWAY. AND LAURA LYONS WAS UNDER HIS INFLUENCE. WHEN SIR HENRY TURNED UP, STAPLETON'S FIRST THOUGHTS WERE TO KILL HIM IN LONDON, SO THAT HE MIGHT NEVER COME TO DARTMOOR AT ALL. IT WAS STAPLETON WE SAW DISGUISED WITH A BEARD IN THE BACK OF THE CARRIAGE. HOWEVER, AFTER MRS. STAPLETON SENT THE WARNING, SIR HENRY WAS EVEN MORE INTENT ON VISITING BASKERVILLE HALL. IN ANTICIPATION OF SIR HENRY'S MURDER, STAPLETON STOLE HIS BOOT. BUT THE NEW BOOT TAKEN FIRST WAS USELESS FOR THIS PURPOSE. HE NEEDED ONE THAT CONTAINED A SCENT FOR THE HOUND, WHICH IS WHY HE STOLE A SECOND, OLD BOOT. AS FOR THE HOUND ITSELF, IT WAS SIMPLY A LARGE DOG THAT STAPLETON COVERED IN PHOSPHOROUS IN ORDER TO GIVE IT A GHOSTLY GLOW.

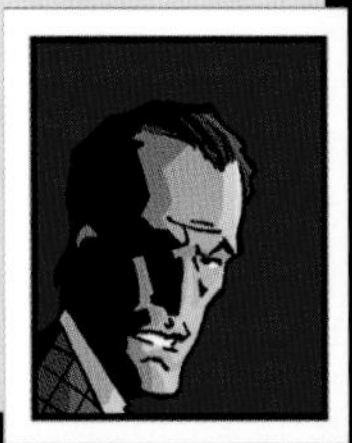

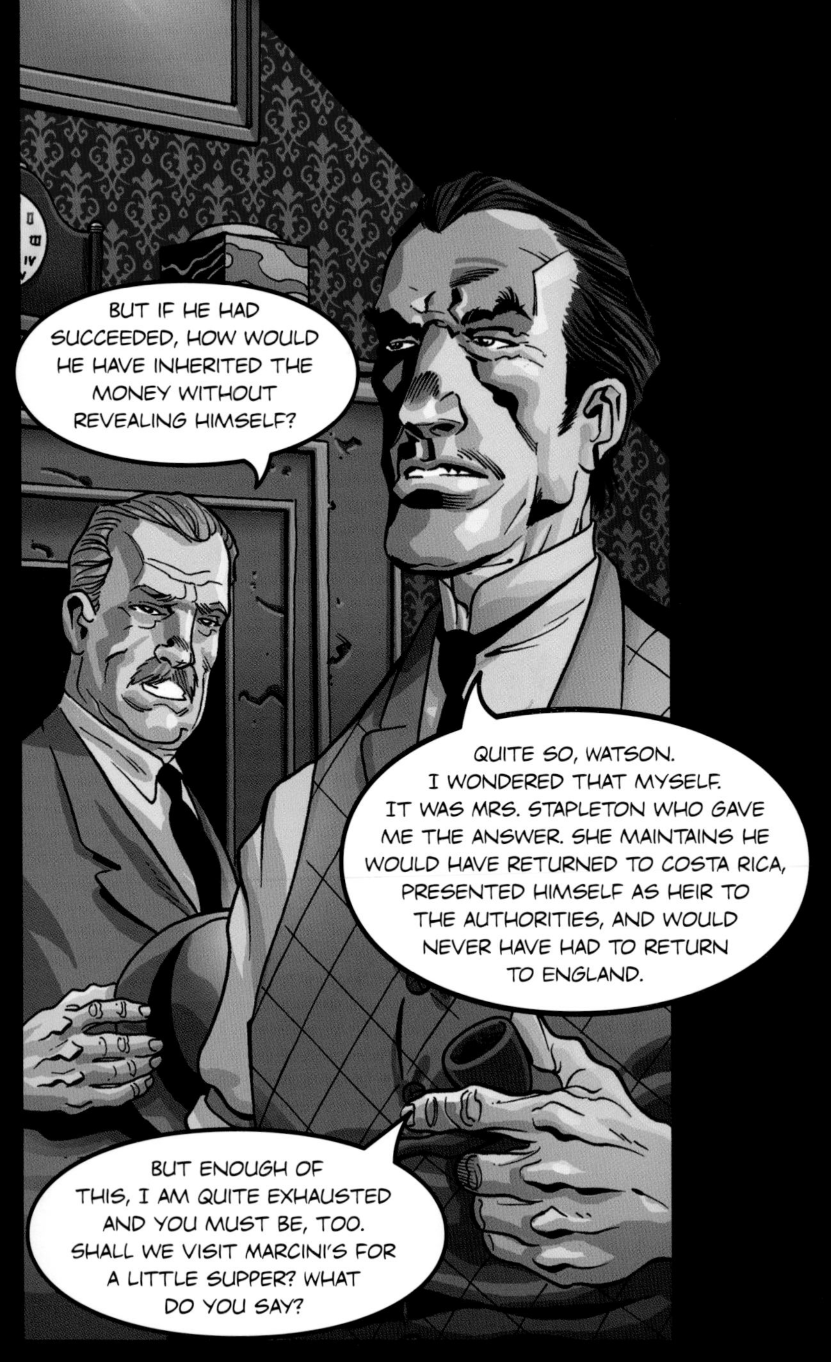
BUT IF HE HAD SUCCEEDED, HOW WOULD HE HAVE INHERITED THE MONEY WITHOUT REVEALING HIMSELF?
QUITE SO, WATSON. I WONDERED THAT MYSELF. IT WAS MRS. STAPLETON WHO GAVE ME THE ANSWER. SHE MAINTAINS HE WOULD HAVE RETURNED TO COSTA RICA, PRESENTED HIMSELF AS HEIR TO THE AUTHORITIES, AND WOULD NEVER HAVE HAD TO RETURN TO ENGLAND.
BUT ENOUGH OF THIS, I AM QUITE EXHAUSTED AND YOU MUST BE, TOO. SHALL WE VISIT MARCINI'S FOR A LITTLE SUPPER? WHAT DO YOU SAY?

PUBLISHED IN 2020 BY
THE ROSEN PUBLISHING GROUP, INC.
29 EAST 21ST STREET, NEW YORK, NY 10010

CATALOGING-IN-PUBLICATION DATA

NAMES: DOYLE, ARTHUR CONAN. | BAMPTON, CLAIRE.
TITLE: THE HOUND OF THE BASKERVILLES / SIR ARTHUR CONAN DOYLE AND CLAIRE BAMPTON.
DESCRIPTION: NEW YORK : POWERKIDS PRESS, 2020. | SERIES: GRAPHIC NOVEL CLASSICS
IDENTIFIERS: ISBN 9781725306332 (PBK.) | ISBN 9781725306349 (LIBRARY BOUND) | ISBN 9781725306387 (6PACK)
SUBJECTS: LCSH: DOYLE, ARTHUR CONAN, 1859-1930. HOUND OF THE BASKERVILLES--ADAPTATIONS. | HOLMES, SHERLOCK--COMIC BOOKS, STRIPS, ETC. | HOLMES, SHERLOCK--JUVENILE FICTION. | WATSON, JOHN H. (FICTITIOUS CHARACTER)--COMIC BOOKS, STRIPS, ETC. | WATSON, JOHN H. (FICTITIOUS CHARACTER)--JUVENILE FICTION. | DOYLE, ARTHUR CONAN, 1859-1930. HOUND OF THE BASKERVILLES--ADAPTATIONS.
CLASSIFICATION: LCC PZ7.7.P69 HO 2019 | DDC 741.5'973--DC23

STORY: CLAIRE **BAMPTON**
ART: ANTHONY **WILLIAMS**
COLOR: ROB **TAYLOR**

MANUFACTURED IN THE UNITED STATES OF AMERICA

CPSIA COMPLIANCE INFORMATION: BATCH CSPK19: FOR FURTHER INFORMATION CONTACT ROSEN PUBLISHING, NEW YORK, NEW YORK AT 1-800-237-9932.